I0663012

LADY GUNSMITH

7

Roxy Doyle and the James Boys

Books by J.R. Roberts
(Robert J. Randisi)

Lady Gunsmith series
The Legend of Roxy Doyle
The Three Graves of Roxy Doyle
Roxy Doyle and The Shanghai Saloon
Roxy Doyle and The Traveling Circus Show
The Portrait of Gavin Doyle
Roxy Doyle and the Desperate Housewife
Roxy Doyle and the James Boys

The Gunsmith series

Angel Eyes series

Tracker series

Mountain Jack Pike series

Coming Soon!
Lady Gunsmith 8
Roxy Doyle and the Silver Queen

For more information visit:
www.SpeakingVolumes.us

LADY GUNSMITH

7

Roxy Doyle and the James Boys

J.R. Roberts

SPEAKING VOLUMES, LLC
NAPLES, FLORIDA
2019

Roxy Doyle and the James Boys

ISBN 978-1-62815-974-5

Chapter One

St. Joseph, Missouri

Roxy Doyle's specialty had sadly become running down rumors of her father's presence in different parts of the country. She couldn't afford to ignore any of them if she was going to someday find Gavin Doyle. So when she heard that the bounty hunter had been seen near St. Joseph, Missouri, off she went.

Of late she had been stuck riding a nine-year-old nag, which had been all she could afford at the time she bought the animal. The horse just made it to St. Joe, and she knew she was going to need a new one, but that wouldn't be until she left town.

Horses weren't important to Roxy. She never named them, because she never expected to have them for very long. And she'd already had this one too long. She was just grateful it had gotten her this far.

"He's on his last legs," the old hostler told her, when she stopped in a livery stable.

"Don't I know it," Roxy said.

"I got a few out back you could look at if you want to buy a new one," he offered.

"I'll take you up on that when I'm ready to leave town," she said.

"Sounds good," he said. "Meanwhile, I'll try to keep this one from fallin' over."

She was becoming fond of older men like this one because they didn't undress her with their eyes.

"Can you recommend a cheap but clean hotel?" she asked him.

"Cheap *and* clean?" he asked. "Those are tough to come by, but try the Hanover Hotel over on Lafayette."

"Lafayette, thanks."

"Can't miss it," he said. "Go out here to the right and walk three blocks."

"Thanks."

She grabbed her rifle and saddlebags and left the livery.

On the three block walk she passed a café, a saloon, a bank, and several other stores. St. Joseph looked to be a bustling community. As usual, the men and women she passed gave her looks, both curious and admiring.

She came to the Hanover Hotel and wasn't disappointed. It looked respectable. Inside, she found the lobby to be fairly clean.

At the desk the young clerk undressed her with his eyes and asked, "Can I help you, Miss?"

"A room, please," she said.

"Certainly. We have a few. What would you like?"

"Just something off the main street," she said.

"Room five," he said, putting the key on the desk. "Would you sign the register, please?"

She signed ROXY DOYLE and left the address blank.

"Do you need help carrying anything up?" he asked, hopefully. "I can take those saddlebags for you—"

"No, I'm fine," she said. "But I would like a bath."

"Hot or cold?"

"Oh, hot," she said.

"When, Miss?"

"As soon as you can get it ready."

"Is ten minutes soon enough?"

"That's fine. I'll be back down for it."

"It'll be ready, Miss . . ." he looked at the register. ". . . . Doyle. I promise."

"Thank you."

She went to the stairs, very aware of him watching her go up. For every hostler, who didn't look at her like a piece of meat, there were always ten hotel desk clerks like this one.

She entered her room, set aside her saddlebags, went to the window to make sure there was no access from outside. It was overlooking an alley, which worked for her.

She went downstairs for her bath.

The desk clerk was entirely too willing to be helpful. In the end, Roxy got him to give her soap and a towel, and direct her to the room where her bath was.

"I can come in and help—" he offered.

"I'll be fine," she said.

"I can bring more hot water—"

"No need," she assured him. "I'll be in and out before the water gets tepid."

She had no desire to soak, she just wanted to get all the trail dust off her, and put on some clean clothes—or, at least, a fresh shirt.

There was one chair in the room with her, and a lock on the door. She had a choice of putting the back of the chair under the doorknob to secure the door or put it near the tub and hang her gunbelt on it. The clerk probably had a key to the room, but she preferred to keep her gun close. If he used to key to come in, he'd be sorry.

Chapter Two

After her bath, Roxy left the hotel, to the obvious disappointment of the clerk. She hoped he wasn't going to be a problem. She had dealt with lovesick young men before, and often they became an annoyance.

She headed back the way she had come and found the small café again. As she entered, she was glad to see that she'd be dealing with a waitress, and not a waiter.

The place was fairly empty as they were between mealtimes, so the waitress said, "Just sit anywhere you like, hon."

Roxy took a back table, and when the waitress asked if she wanted a menu, she replied, "What's the special?"

"Pork chops today," the woman said. "With potatoes and green beans."

"I'll take it," Roxy said.

"And to drink?"

"Can I get a beer?"

"Of course," the woman said. "Comin' up."

She brought the beer first, and then the special on a steaming plate.

"Enjoy," the woman said. "First special of the day."

"Thank you."

As she ate, she was able to look out the front door and the window at people passing by, and could see a bank across the street. While she watched, she saw the bank door open and a man step out. She dropped her fork and hurried to the window for a better look.

"Is everything okay?" the waitress asked.

"Oh, yeah, fine," Roxy said. "I just thought I saw somebody I know."

"Oh? I know a lot of people in town. Who did you see?"

"That man in front of the bank?" Roxy said. "Wearing a grey suit, and hat—"

"Oh, that's Mr. Howard."

"Howard?" Roxy asked.

"Thomas Howard," the woman said. "Him and his wife, they've eaten here a time or two."

"I see," Roxy said, going back to her table. The waitress followed her. "Has he lived here long?"

"A couple of months, I think," the woman said. "Him and his wife bought a house down at the end of Lafayette, where it becomes—residential, they called it."

"Howard," Roxy said.

"Is that who you thought you saw?" the woman asked.

"No," Roxy said, "I don't know anybody named Howard. Guess I was wrong."

"When did you get to town?" the woman asked.

"Today," Roxy said. "Just passing through."

"Then it'd be a real coincidence for you to see somebody you knew."

"Yeah, it would," Roxy said.

A man and a woman entered and the waitress went to seat them, leaving Roxy to enjoy her meal.

***

After eating Roxy paid her bill. Several other tables had become occupied, so the waitress wasn't trying to make conversation anymore, which was fine with Roxy. She was still puzzled about the man she had seen come out of the bank.

The waitress said the man lived with his wife at the end of Lafayette Street, so Roxy decided to take a stroll in that direction.

When she got to the residential section, she saw several houses with white picket fences and gardens, and wondered which one belonged to the "Howards?"

When there was no movement outside any of the houses, she figured she could come back another time. After all, she was there to check on the rumor that Gavin Doyle was in the area. Checking on "Thomas Howard" could come later.

***

With all the searching she had done over the years, Roxy had come to depend heavily on bartenders to confirm or disprove rumors.

The saloon she had passed walking to her hotel from the livery was called The Horseshoe Saloon, with a big wooden horseshoe over the front door. She decided to start her search there.

Initially, she would have a beer at the bar and listen to conversations going on around her. If that yielded nothing, then she would ask the bartender some questions. And all of this was assuming no drunk idiot tried to talk to her, or touch her, in which case too much attention would be drawn to her when she put that drunk down.

The saloon wasn't half full, as it was still early in the day. Shopkeepers and employees were still minding their stores, and ranch hands were still working their jobs. So there was plenty of room for her at the bar.

The bartender wasn't young, but he wasn't old, either. He gave her an admiring look, but made no lewd remarks. He simply asked, "What'll ya have, Miss?"

"A beer."

"Comin' up."

She kept her back to the room, but used the mirror behind the bar to keep an alert eye out. Men were looking at her, but none were approaching. After a few moments, conversations continued.

The bartender served her beer. She picked it up and sipped it while she listened.

Chapter Three

By the time she had finished her beer, she'd heard nothing interesting or informative. Time to go to plan B.

"Another?" she asked.

"Comin'," the bartender promised.

When he brought it, she said, "Thanks. What's your name?"

"Artie."

"Well, Artie, I'm in St. Joe looking for a man."

"Lots to choose from," he said.

"This is a particular man. I'm wondering if you've seen or heard anything about him."

"Who is he?"

"His name's Gavin Doyle."

"Well, I know the name," Artie said. "A bounty hunter, right?"

"That's right."

"I don't know 'im," Artie said. "Ain't never met 'im."

"Have you heard anything about him being in town?" she asked. "Or near here?"

"Not a word," he said. "Is he huntin' somebody here?"

"Not that I know of."

"Are you huntin' him?" he asked. "Is that it?"

"Not hunting," she said. "Just looking for him."

"Why? What for?"

She hesitated, then said, "He's my father."

"Oh."

"Does that make a difference in what you know?"

"I'm sorry, but no," he said. "I've got no information for you."

"Okay." She drank down half the second beer, pushed the rest away. "Thanks for the drinks. What do I owe you?"

"On the house," he said. "Come on back when you get thirsty again."

"I will."

***

She tried the same tactics at two other saloons, with no luck. There were no revealing conversations, and none of the bartenders had ever served her father a drink or heard that he was in town.

In the last saloon she tried, the clientele were less mannerly, and there were several remarks and whistles thrown her way. She ignored them all, but when she left, she heard someone behind her.

"Hey, girlie," a man's voice called.

She turned, saw a single man standing on the boardwalk in front of the saloon.

"Are you talking to me?" she asked.

"I hear you're lookin' for Gavin Doyle."

"That's right."

"Well," he said, "I kin take you to him."

He was a tall, slovenly looking man, with sweat stains on his clothes and dirty, greasy tendrils of hair drifting out from beneath his equally dirty and sweaty hat.

"Is that a fact?"

"Sure."

"Where is he?"

"It ain't far," the man said. "Fact is, he's been waitin' for you."

"Is that right?" she asked. "How did he know I was coming?"

The man hesitated a moment, and his eyes darted about as he sought an answer.

"I dunno," he said, finally. "He just did. Told me to come to town and look out for ya. And here I am."

"How far is it?" she asked.

"Oh, we can walk," he said. "Ain't that far."

"Okay, then," she said. "Lead the way."

"Sure thing, honey."

She followed him for a few blocks, but when he started to lead her down an alley, she figured they'd gone far enough.

"Hold up, there," she said.

"It's just at the end of this alley," he said, pointing.

"No," she said, "it's not. I don't know what's at the end of the alley, or what you think you've got planned for me, but it's not Gavin Doyle."

He turned to face her. The gun on his hip looked well worn.

"Okay, then," he said, "why don't we do it right here?"

"Do what?"

"Fuck," he said. "What else do you think a man like me wants with a woman like you?"

"Oh, I don't know, maybe a lesson in manners?"

He laughed.

"You're gonna give me a lesson?" he asked.

"I'm going to give you worse than that, friend," she said. "I'm going to shoot a toe off."

He laughed again, then grew serious and said, "Come on and try—"

Before he could get the word "it" out, she drew and fired. The tip of his boot flew off, and with it a toe or two.

"Owwwwww!" he howled, falling down onto his butt and grabbing his foot. "What the hell—you shot off my foot."

"A toe," she said, ejecting the spent shell from her gun and replacing it, "maybe two. I'd get to a doctor if I was you."

"Aw geez . . ." he moaned as she turned and walked out of the alley, ". . . what'd ya go and do that for?"

Chapter Four

Roxy felt that her next move had to be a visit to the local law, if for no other reason than the man whose toe she had shot off might report it.

She didn't know if St. Joe had a sheriff, or a police department, so she walked around town until spotting a brick building. It apparently housed City Hall and the Mayor's Office, as well as the "City Guard."

She went through the front door and saw a uniformed man standing at a desk. He was young, and as she approached, she could see he was being affected by her appearance.

"Can I help you, Miss?" he asked.

"Yes, I'd like to talk to someone who's in charge," she said. "Would that be you?"

"No, Miss," he said. "I'm just a police officer—Officer Bowen. There are a lot of men ahead of me. We have some sergeants, a lieutenant, a captain, and our chief-of-police."

"Then I might as well go right to the chief-of-police," she said.

"Oh, I'm sorry, but he's not here right now," the officer said.

"Okay," she said, "Officer Bowen, what's your first name?"

"I'm Mike, Miss."

"If the Chief isn't here, who is?"

"Captain Kelly, Miss."

"Then could I talk to Captain Kelly?"

"I'll ask, Miss," he said. He started to leave the desk, then turned back to her. "I'll be right back."

"Fine. I'll wait here."

He left the desk, went back into the bowels of the building. When he returned, it was with an older man wearing a uniform with captain's bars.

"Miss," Officer Bowen said, "this is Captain Kelly."

Kelly was a man in his forties, with black-and-grey hair and a firm jaw. He gave Roxy a serious look.

"Miss, can I ask what this is about?"

"I'm in town looking for somebody," she said. "I wanted to see if you could be of any help. Also, there was an incident I thought I should report."

"What sort of incident?" Kelly asked.

"Well," she said, "I shot a man's toe off. Maybe two."

"What?" Kelly asked. Bowen stifled a laugh. "Why would you do that?" The Captain asked.

"He was about to rape me."

Bowen didn't laugh at that.

"Miss," Kelly said, "what's your name?"

"Roxy Doyle," she said.

"All right Miss Doyle," Kelly said, "I think you'd better come back to my office with me."

He started back, with Roxy following, and Bowen coming up behind, but Kelly stopped and said, "Bowen, you stay at the desk."

"Oh," the young officer said, sadly, "yes, sir."

Roxy followed Kelly back into the building, past a few desks until they came to a small office.

"The Chief has the large one at the end," he said, pointing further on, "but he's away, at the moment. Come inside."

They entered the office and Roxy sat in front of the desk that seemed to fill the room, while Kelly took his position behind it.

"Miss Doyle," he said, "I think I recognize your name. You're the one they call Lady Gunsmith?"

"That's right."

"So you felt the need to shoot somebody in the foot?" Kelly asked.

"Captain, can I tell you why I'm in St. Joseph?"

"Please do."

"I'm looking for my father, Gavin Doyle."

"The bounty hunter."

"Right. I heard a rumor that he was in this area, so I came to find out. I talked to some bartenders today, and at one saloon this man followed me out, and told me he'd take me to my father."

"Ah," he said, "so you went with him."

"Against my better judgment," she said. "He led me to an alley, and I called a halt to it, there."

"Then you shot him."

"I called him on his lie," she said, "and he turned and said he was going to have me."

"Rape?"

"I didn't wait to find out," she said. "I told him if he tried anything, I'd shoot off a toe."

"And you did."

"I could've killed him."

"I understand that," he said. "Do you know who the man was?"

"No," she said, "but you probably won't have any trouble finding him. He'll be the one limping around town."

"All right," he said. "So other than that, you'd like to know if we've heard anything about Gavin Doyle being in the area."

"That's right."

"Well, I'm afraid the answer to that is, no."

"Can you speak for all your officers?"

"Obviously not," he said. "All right, I'll ask them all if they've heard anything."

"Thank you."

"Meanwhile," he went on, "the rest of the time you're here, I'd appreciate it if you didn't shoot anymore citizens in the foot."

"Agreed."

"Or kill any."

"I'm not planning on killing anyone," she said.

"That's good."

"That is," she added, "anyone who doesn't force me into it."

"Let me walk you out."

He walked her back to the front door.

"I'll check with my men as I see them," he promised.

"Thanks," she said. "I'll check back with you . . . tomorrow?"

"Sure, why not?" he said. "I won't have spoken to all of them by then, but many."

"Okay," she said. "I appreciate the help."

She stepped outside the building, stopped and took a moment to consider her next move.

Chapter Five

She decided to take the time to find out about Mister Thomas Howard.

If he was who she thought he was, there was no way she could ask the Chief-of-Police or the Captain, or any policeman, about him. She just had to get a better look at the man, and that meant going back to his house.

She took the walk over there, keeping alert in case he was on the street. She also had to stay aware in case of trouble or, if it should happen, her father was on the street. Of course, that last one was just too much to ask for. After years of searching, it wasn't likely he was just going to walk up to her on the street. One of the things Clint Adams had taught her years ago was not to depend on coincidences.

When she reached the Howard house, she saw that the address was 1318 Lafayette Street. She could always go to the office where they filed deeds and see whose name was on it. But she would save that for later. Now she would just take a chance on getting a clear look at him.

There was an apparently abandoned house right across the street, with overgrown bushes blocking a view of the porch. She went up on that porch and positioned herself so she could see the front door of 1318, but nobody from the street could see her.

And she waited.

***

Officer Mike Bowen was jolted from his reverie when he saw the man limping into the station. He knew his name was Tom Cameron, and he knew this was the man Roxy Doyle had been talking about.

"I got a report to make," Cameron said, his voice tinged with pain.

"About what?" Bowen asked.

"Some bitch shot my toe off," he complained.

"Yeah?" Mike Bowen asked. "And what did you do to deserve it?"

"Huh? I didn't do nothin'!" he exclaimed. "I didn't do one damn thing to her."

"That's not the way she told it."

"She's been here, already?"

"She sure has," Bowen said, leaning forward on his desk. "She reported that you tried to rape her, so if I was you, I'd get the hell out of here."

"That lyin' bitch!"

"You're the liar, Cameron," Bowen said. "That's your reputation, and I believe you're living up to it. If you want my advice, you'll leave that woman alone, or you'll have to deal with me."

"So you ain't gonna do your job and arrest her?" Cameron complained.

"If I do my job, Cameron, that means I've got to throw you into a cell and charge you with attempted rape," Bowen said. "You want that?"

"I don't gotta rape women, you know," Cameron grumbled.

"Yeah, I know," Bowen said. "You pay them."

"Now look—"

"Get out of here, Cameron!"

Cameron limped painfully out of the building, muttering to himself.

Mike Bowen went back to thinking about Roxy Doyle, the Lady Gunsmith, who he was already in love with.

***

Roxy was about to quit when the front door of 1318 opened and the man stepped out. He was the one the waitress had told her was Thomas Howard. She got a real good look at him, this time, as he came walking down the path to the street.

The people in St. Joe might know him as Thomas Howard, but she now knew for a fact that he was Jesse James.

Chapter Six

She didn't risk following him. Jesse would probably spot her, because he was bound to be on the alert, just as she was, when walking the streets. She wondered if Frank James was also in St. Joe, living under an assumed name? The first time she had met Frank, he was living as somebody else, and they had gotten together before she found out who he really was. She had been introduced to Jesse by Belle Starr, when Belle was trying to recruit Roxy for her gang. She didn't join the Outlaw Queen, but they became friends.

She couldn't claim to have become friends with Jesse James, but he would know who she was if he saw her. If they ran into each other on the street it was going to be awkward. She needed to let him know she was there.

When she first met Jesse, she knew he was married to his cousin Zee, but had not met the woman. She decided maybe that was the way to go, so she left the porch of the abandoned house, and crossed over to 1318.

She went up the path to the front door and knocked. It was answered by a pleasant looking blonde woman who was wiping her hands on the apron she wore around her waist.

"Yes?"

"Are you Mrs. Howard?"

"That's right."

"My name is Roxy Doyle."

She waited for the name to strike the woman, but apparently it didn't.

"Yes?"

"Mrs. Howard," she said, "I know your husband."

"Is that right? When did you meet him?"

"Some time back, when I was riding with Belle Starr," Roxy said. "Only, when I met him, his name was Jesse James."

The woman tried to maintain her composure, but Roxy could see she was shaken.

"I don't know what—"

"Mrs. Howard," she said, "I don't want Jesse to see me walking down the street and be surprised. I want to let him know I'm here, and that I'm not going to say a word about who he really is."

The woman obviously didn't know what to do.

"If I could come in," Roxy said. "Maybe you've heard of me under another name? Some folks call me Lady Gunsmith."

Zee's eyes widened.

"Oh," she said, "Roxy Doyle. Of course! Well, you may as well come in."

"Thank you."

She led Roxy into the clean, well-kept house. The furniture was solid, but not expensive looking. If Jesse had any of the money he had stolen from trains and banks over the years, he hadn't spent it on the house.

"Would you like something? We just finished supper. I could put something together for you."

"Let's talk first, and then see if you still want to feed me," Roxy suggested.

"All right. Please, have a seat."

They both sat, Zee on the sofa, Roxy in a matching chair.

"Your name is Zee, right?" Roxy asked.

"I suppose there's no point in lying to you," the woman said. "Yes, I'm Zee—Zerelda, actually—although these days I answer to Mrs. Howard."

"Zee, I'm really not here to cause anyone any trouble," Roxy said. "I heard a rumor that my father was seen near here and came to look into it."

"Your father is Gavin Doyle, right? Yes, Jesse told me about meeting you with Belle, and about your father."

"I saw Jesse on the street earlier, and someone told me he was Thomas Howard."

"Yes, he took that name a couple of years ago when we were in Nashville with Frank."

"What name did Frank take?"

"He was—and still is—B.J. Woodson."

"Is he also living in St. Joe?"

"No, when we came here to settle, Frank decided to go to Virginia. Jesse and me, we're just more comfortable in Missouri."

"Well, like I said, I don't want Jesse to see me on the street and be surprised," Roxy explained. "So if you could tell him I'm here, and that I'm at the Hanover Hotel, he doesn't even have to come and see me. I just want you both to know you have nothing to fear from me. Your secret is safe."

"I appreciate that, Roxy," Zee said, "and I'm sure Jesse will, too. But why don't you let me make you a plate, and you can eat and wait here for Jesse to come back and tell him yourself. He won't be gone long. He just went to get some tobacco."

"Well," Roxy said, "A home-cooked meal would go down real good."

"It's settled, then," Zee said, getting to her feet. "I'll feed you and we'll get to know each other better, until Jesse gets back."

Chapter Seven

Zee laid out a plate of fried chicken for Roxy, with carrots and potatoes, then sat across the kitchen table from her as she ate. They talked and ended up laughing together and liking each other. Roxy was eating a piece of apple pie with coffee when they heard the front door open.

Zee got to her feet right away.

"Let me warn him before he comes in here and sees you," she said.

"Good idea."

But Roxy wondered if the warning was so that Jesse would be able to walk in holding a gun. Roxy pushed her chair back so she would be able to get to her gun quickly, if the need arose. But she hoped it wouldn't.

She heard the voices from the other room, and then Zee was the first to enter the kitchen. As Jesse came in behind her, Roxy tensed, prepared for the worst, but as he came into view, his hands were empty.

"Roxy Doyle," he said, with a smile.

"Thomas Howard, I presume," Roxy said, standing.

They shook hands, rather awkwardly.

"Thomas," Zee said, "why don't you sit and I'll pour you some coffee?"

"Good idea," he said, then to Roxy, "Sit, let's talk."

Jesse sat across from Roxy and Zee put a cup of coffee in front of him, then sat.

"Zee told me what you said," Jesse commented. "We appreciate it that you're willin' to keep quiet."

"Why wouldn't I?" Roxy asked. "What you want to do with your life is your business."

"We're settlin' down," Jesse said. "No more banks, no more trains . . . once the gang got whittled down to just me and Frank, we decided to retire—us here, Frank in Virginia."

"I'm sorry to miss seeing Frank," Roxy said, "but I'm glad he's happy."

"Oh, he is," Jesse said.

"Is he married?"

"No," Jesse said, "he lives by himself, and he likes it that way."

Roxy looked at Zee, wondering if she knew about her dalliance with Frank James?

"How long do you plan on stayin' in St. Joe?" Jesse asked.

"Not long," Roxy said. "I just have to make sure my father's not here, and then I'll move on."

"I can ask around town, see what I can find out," Jesse said.

"No, don't do that," Roxy said. "Don't give people any reason to wonder about you. Asking about a bounty hunter might attract the kind of attention you don't want."

"You're right about that. Thanks."

Roxy looked at Zee.

"Thank you for the meal, Zee. It was delicious."

Roxy stood up, and Jesse stood with her.

"I'll walk Roxy to the door, Zee," he said.

"I hope to see you again, Roxy," Zee said.

"I'll say goodbye before I leave town, Mrs. Howard," Roxy said.

Zee smiled.

"You do that," she said.

Jesse walked with Roxy to the front door, opened it for her, then lowered his voice.

"Zee says you're at the Hanover?"

"That's right."

"I'll want to talk to you, later or tomorrow. Is that okay?"

"Sure, Jess—Mr. Howard," Roxy said. "What about?"

"Not now," he said. "I'll come and see you."

"Okay," Roxy said, "I'll be waiting."

As she stepped outside, and Jesse closed the door behind her, Roxy hoped Jesse didn't want what most men wanted from her, not with a wife like Zee.

***

Roxy went to her hotel and directly to her room, rather than go to a saloon and take a chance on another slovenly man taking a run at her. She preferred to sit in her room, think about Jesse and Zee James—or Mr. and Mrs. Howard—assuming their new lives here in St. Joe, and whether or not her father was anywhere in the vicinity.

She locked her door and pushed the back of a wooden chair beneath the doorknob, as a double lock. The window was far enough off the ground and had no access, so she didn't have to worry about that. And it looked out on an alley, so there was no rooftop across from her, or window, that somebody could use to take a shot at her from.

All of that done, she removed her gunbelt and hung it on the bedpost, then removed her boots and reclined on the bed, still dressed. Since there was a chance "Thomas Howard" might come to see her, she decided to keep her clothes on. Although Jesse James had made no attempts to woo her the first time they met, she didn't want to give him any ideas. And she knew she gave men ideas, without even trying. It was a sort of curse, which she had suffered since her early teens. Sometimes she thought she should cut her red locks off and gain fifty pounds. Then she could take care of business without men making fools of themselves over her.

She drifted off to sleep . . .

Chapter Eight

The knock abruptly woke her. She sat straight up, grabbed her gun and almost put a bullet through the door.

She carried the gun to the door with her.

"Who is it?"

"Thomas Howard."

She cracked the door, saw that it was, indeed, Jesse James, and opened it wide.

"Let me in before somebody sees me," he said.

"Sure, come on in."

She backed away for him to enter, then closed the door.

"Anybody see you come into the hotel?" she asked.

"No, I used the back," Jesse said. "Thanks for letting me in. Did I wake you?"

"I was just dozing," she said, walking to the bedpost and holstering her gun. "Does Zee know you're here?"

"No."

That raised a red flag for Roxy. She remained where she was, standing at the head of the bed, with her gun in easy reach. "What's on your mind, Jesse?" she asked. "Or should I call you Thomas?"

"No, when we're alone, Jesse's okay."

"So Jesse, what's up?"

"I want to recruit you, Roxy."

"For what?"

"What else?" he asked. "The new James gang."

"But I thought you were settling down?"

"That's what I told Zee," Jesse said. "But I'm not done. And I don't think Frank is, either."

"So Frank's in this new gang?"

"Not yet," Jesse said, "but he will be, when I contact him."

"Jesse—"

"Why else are you here, Roxy?" Jesse asked. "This can't be just a coincidence, you're supposed to be here. This is fate, girl."

"Jesse . . . I'm still looking for my father."

"I'm not gonna stop you from doin' that, Roxy," Jesse said. "I just need you in the gang so when I go to recruit others, I can tell them you're in. You are in, ain'tcha?"

"I'm sorry, Jesse, I'm not looking to join a gang," Roxy said. "As much as I hate to say it, it is a coincidence that I'm here."

"Look, I've got the Ford boys here, and they're in. Will you do me a favor and think it over?"

"Sure, I'll think it over, Jesse."

"Give me your final answer when you're ready to leave town."

"Agreed."

"But for now," he said, "Zee isn't expectin' me back for a while. What do you say you and me—"

"Jesse," Roxy said. "Tell me you're kidding."

He stared at her a moment, then grinned and said, "Yeah, of course I'm kiddin', Roxy. Come on, I'm a married man!"

"You see, I knew that," Roxy said, "and if you weren't, we'd be in the bed right now."

"But Zee would kill me," he said, "so I'm gonna get out of here. Think about what I just offered you. A chance to be in the new James gang with not only me, but Frank."

"I will, Jesse," she said, trying like hell not to insult him, because she knew what his temper used to be like. She just didn't know if "Thomas Howard" had the same temper. "Thanks for the offer."

"Sure," Jesse said. "Frank and me and the Fords, we'd love to have ya."

"The Fords are . . ."

"Bob and Charley," he said. "Charley rode with us before, but Bob's new."

"Okay, Jesse," she said, "you'll have my answer probably in a couple of days."

"Good enough, Roxy," Jesse said.

As he went to the door she said, "I do have one piece of advice, if you don't mind taking it from somebody younger than you."

"Go ahead."

"Tell Zee what you're planning," Roxy said. "Don't make her believe you're going to settle down, only to disappoint her. Let her be in on it with you."

"I'll consider it," he said, and slipped quickly out of the room.

***

Roxy spent the rest of the night thinking about Jesse's offer and how to turn him down without having him take it personally. She had seen him kill a man in a fit of rage, and she didn't want to have to go up against him. Though many people in Missouri thought of him as a legend and a hero, Roxy considered him to be an expert with a gun, and a born killer. Having to go against him would be daunting, and having to kill him would break her heart.

Chapter Nine

In the morning she returned to the café down the street for breakfast. The Hanover did not have its own diningroom. During breakfast, she went over the short meeting she'd had with Jesse James in her room the night before. Probably the best way to handle Jesse was to lie to him, tell him she got a line on her father's whereabouts, and had to leave town.

But that wouldn't be until she actually was ready to leave town. Before she did that, she'd have to talk with Captain Kelly, see if any of his men had heard anything about Gavin Doyle.

That would happen later in the day. She needed something to do until then, rather than just sitting around waiting for something to happen.

Then she remembered that she needed to buy a new horse. The hostler had told her he had a few in a corral behind the livery. She decided to go and take a look.

***

"There you go," the hostler said. "Take your pick."

She had gone back to the livery where she'd left her horse, and the man was only too willing to let her have a look at the mounts he had available.

There were six horses in the corral, and they all looked fairly fit to her. All she needed was an animal that would get her out of St. Joe, and not fall apart when things got a little rough.

"What about that one?" she asked, pointing.

"The roan? He's six years old. I just got him last week from a man who needed the money."

"I'd like him, but I don't know if I can afford him," Roxy said.

"We can work somethin' out," he said. "Your horse is a little worn out, but he ain't so bad."

If he was a little younger, she would have been suspicious regarding the man's comment about "working things out," but he seemed sincere.

"Let's talk about it," he suggested, and they went back inside.

***

By the time she left the livery, she had a new horse. It took most of the money she had left in her poke, which meant she was going to have to look for some kind of job soon, so she could continue her search.

But for now, she had a room and a horse, and a few dollars left to eat with. Then she remembered Jesse James' offer. She didn't know when he was planning his first job with his new gang, but maybe just one would serve to outfit her for a while.

Many residents of Missouri looked at Jesse James as a sort of Robin Hood figure, only stealing from those who could afford it, like banks and railroads. Thinking that way, she might be able to justify going with him on just one job. But would he accept that?

She was walking back to her hotel when she heard the shot and felt the burn in her left shoulder. The bullet actually punched her, pushing her forward, and she went with it, hitting the ground, rolling and finding cover behind a horse trough before a second shot could be fired.

People on the street ducked for cover, but when a second shot wasn't forthcoming, they began to leave the area. Soon the street was deserted, except for Roxy, sitting on the ground with her back against the side of the trough.

That was the last thing she remembered . . .

***

When she awoke, she was staring at a white ceiling. As she started to rise, firm hands pushed her back down.

"Take it easy," a man's voice said. "You've been shot, but you're all right."

"Where am I?"

"My office," the man said. "I'm Doctor Willoughby."

"How did I get here?"

"One of our police officers brought you in."

She looked up at the grey-haired man who was speaking to her.

"How bad?"

"Not bad, at all. It didn't go all the way through, or you'd be bleeding from the front and the back. I got the bullet out and bandaged your shoulder. I don't think it hit anything vital. You should be able to move your arm, flex your fingers."

"Left side?" she asked.

"That's right."

She flexed the fingers of her left hand, then tried to move her arm. It hurt, but it moved.

"There," he said, "you're okay. Do you want to sit up now?"

"Yes."

"Let me help you."

He supported her with his hand behind her back and got her to a seated position.

"Where's the police officer who brought me in?" she asked, feeling a little dizzy.

"Just outside, I'll bring him in," Doc Willoughby said. "He wants to talk to you."

"I want to talk to him, too."

The doctor left the room.

When Officer Mike Bowen entered, she recognized him right away.

Chapter Ten

"I was a block away and heard the shot," he told her, "so I came running. When I saw it was you, I picked you up and carried you here."

Luckily, he was a strong young man, because she knew her dead weight would have been heavy.

"I appreciate it," she said. "You probably saved my life."

"I doubt that," he said. "The Doc said you were gonna be all right. Do you know who shot you?"

"Not a clue," she said.

"How many shots were there?"

"Just the one," she said. "I took cover after that. I guess the shooter got discouraged and lit out."

"Well," Bowen said, "we don't take very kindly to havin' visitors in our town shot on our streets. I'm sure the Chief will have somebody lookin' into it."

"Not you?"

"Me? Hell, no. I just man the desk. I was actually on my way home when this happened."

"Well, thanks to you, I'm all patched up," she said. "I'll tell your chief how much I appreciate it."

"Thanks," Bowen said. "Maybe I can get out from behind that desk."

"I guess I better settle up with the doc," she said. "It'll probably take the last of my funds."

"Don't worry about it," Bowen said. "I brought you in, so the city will take care of it."

"Really? Thank you, Mike."

He seemed pleased that she remembered his name.

"Doc says you can leave. Do you need help gettin' back to your hotel?"

"I think I do," she said. "Maybe I could just lean on you?"

"Sure thing," he said. "Come on, I'll help you up."

She put her right arm around his shoulder, but once they got outside, she was going to want to keep that arm free. He walked her to the outer office, and the door, and the doctor told her to come back the next day so he could check her bandage.

"Thank you, Doc," she said.

On the street Bowen put an arm around her waist, freeing her gun arm and they walked to the hotel that way. He was, indeed, a tall, strong young man, and seemed to handle her weight easily.

When they got to the hotel, the desk clerk came running out to her.

"I heard what happened, Miss. Can I help?"

"I'm all right," she assured him. "The Officer, here, was very helpful."

The clerk watched Bowen help Roxy up the stairs, and was very envious, and jealous.

They moved down the hall together, and then he slid his arm from around her, took her key and unlocked the door. He helped her inside, and to the bed, where she sat. For a moment she was dizzy, but it passed.

"Can I do anythin' else for you?" he asked.

"You can close the door."

He went to the door, started to step out into the hall.

"No, from the inside."

"Oh." He stepped back in and closed the door.

"Could you help me with my gunbelt?"

"Sure."

He knelt in front of her, bringing their faces close together, and undid her belt.

"Just hang it there," she said, indicating the bed post.

"Sure."

She could see some sweat on his brow, and thought it was from nerves. She found that endearing.

"I feel like I need to do something to thank you," she said.

"I was just doin' my job—"

"Still." She put her right hand on his cheek, then slid it around behind his head to draw him to her. She kissed him, flicking her tongue out just a bit. It was not odd that being shot made her feel like sex. It was a reaction to still being alive.

But her shoulder wound kept them from doing anything but kissing, for now.

"Thank you, Mike," she said, as they broke the kiss.

"Um, oh, sure," he said, his eyes glassy.

"Maybe you should go and tell your captain what happened," she said, "so he can have someone check into it."

"Oh, yeah," he said, standing. "He'll probably send somebody to see you. We actually have a detective in our department."

"Well," she said, "that should be interesting."

He walked to the door, then turned back.

"Would you mind if I came by again? I mean, just to check on you."

"Not only don't I mind," she said, "I insist on it."

Maybe later she would be ready for more than kissing.

"I'll see you then," he said, and left.

She tested her hand and arm, found that she could move them both, albeit painfully. She decided to see if she could get some rest, but first she got up and moved the wooden chair to put the back of it beneath the doorknob.

She didn't need any more surprises.

Chapter Eleven

Roxy woke lying on her right side, which she never did. It tended to pin her right arm beneath her, leading to the possibility of it falling asleep. If someone broke into her room at that point, she'd never been able to draw her gun.

But she couldn't lie on her injured left side, so this was going to have to do for now. If she could, she'd try to keep the right arm free.

As she got herself to a seated position, her left side felt stiff. She needed to stand and loosen up a bit. The knock came at the door as she was walking around. She grabbed her gun and went to answer it.

"Who is it?"

"Miss Doyle, I'm Detective Ed Nelson. Captain Kelly sent me to talk to you."

She used her left hand to turn the doorknob and open the door a crack. As she eyed him, the detective looked back at her and smiled.

"I'm alone, I assure you."

She opened the door and backed away.

"Come on in," she said. "I can't be too careful."

"Especially after what happened today," the man said. "I understand."

Detective Nelson was shorter than she was and had a very sad face. As he removed his hat, she saw that he also had a pair of oversized ears.

"Ed Nelson," he said. "I'm pleased to meet you."

"Do you mind if I sit?" she asked. "I'm still not that steady."

"That's fine," he said. "Can I help you?"

"No, I'm fine." She went to the bed, holstered the gun, and sat.

"I'm workin' on findin' out who fired that shot at you," he said. "I talked to some of the people on the street, and in that neighborhood. So far I haven't come up with anythin'."

"I didn't think you would," she said. "These kind of people make sure they're not seen."

"Well, I'm not ready to give up," he said. "I wanted to see you, first, to make sure you're all right . . ."

"I am," she said.

". . . and second, to see if there was anythin' else you remembered."

"I'm afraid not," she said. "The bullet was a complete shock."

"Really?" he asked. "With your reputation, don't you expect this sort of thing?"

"Of course," she said, "but it's still a shock to have a bullet slam into your body."

"I suppose it is," he said. "I've never experienced it."

"I hope you never do."

"That's—well, that's, uh, nice of you to say," he said. "Uh, do you happen to know anyone in town?"

"Not a soul."

"The captain told me you're here looking for your father, Gavin Doyle?"

"That's right."

"He asked me to pass on a message," Nelson said. "Nobody in our department has heard anything about Doyle being in this area."

"I see," she said. "Tell the Captain thank you, for me."

"So you'll probably want to be on your way."

"I would," she said, "if somebody hadn't shot me."

"Oh, right," he said, "you'll need time to heal."

"And to find the shooter."

"Well, I'll be working on that."

"And I appreciate it," she said, "but I'll probably be looking into it myself."

"And by that do you mean, finding the culprit and killing him?"

"I mean finding him," she said. "What happens then, well, we'll just have to see, won't we?"

"I'll let my captain know how you feel about it," Nelson said. "Thank you for seeing me."

He walked to the door, put his hand on the knob, then turned back.

"Is there anything else I can do for you?"

"No, thank you, Detective," she said. "I'm satisfied that you're doing your job."

He nodded, put his hat on, and left the room.

***

After the detective left, she replaced the chair beneath the door knob. It was dark out now, and she was hungry, but she wasn't ready to go back out, just yet. She hoped the young officer, Mike Bowen, had been serious about checking up on her, because if he showed up, she'd ask him to go and get her something to eat. Failing that, she would go downstairs and ask the desk clerk. He was very anxious to do something—anything—for her.

Chapter Twelve

This time when the knock came, Roxy was sure it was Mike Bowen, but she took her gun to the door, anyway.

"Who is it?"

"Mike Bowen."

She opened the door for him, confident he would be alone. Not only was she right, but he was carrying a tray of food.

"I thought you'd be hungry," he said, entering the room.

"You're brilliant!" she said, and kissed him quickly, knowing there was going to be more to come later.

The tray was covered with a napkin, and when he removed it, she saw two plates.

"I thought we'd eat together," he said. "I hope you don't mind."

"Not if you brought something to drink."

"I couldn't bring any beer, but I have this." He took a flask from his back pocket.

"That'll do," she said.

"And I brought beef stew so you could eat it with one hand, if you had to."

"You're impressing me with your brain and your smile, Mike," she said.

His smile broadened at that, and they started to eat.

***

Thomas Howard entered his house on Lafayette Street, and Zee could see something was wrong.

"Jesse? What happened?"

"I just heard from Bob Ford," he said. "Roxy's been shot."

"What?"

"Somebody bushwhacked her on the street."

"Jesse . . ."

He glared at his wife.

"It wasn't me! Why would I shoot 'er?" he shouted.

"She recognized you."

"So what? I accepted her word that she's not gonna say anythin'. Why would I shoot 'er? Jeez, Zee . . ."

"I'm sorry," she said. "Who else in town would have reason to shoot her?"

"Anybody who wants to make a name for themselves by killing Lady Gunsmith"

"I guess you're right. Is she okay?"

"Word is Doc Willoughby patched her up and she's in her hotel."

"You should check on her."

"Thomas Howard can't be seen visiting Lady Gunsmith," he told her.

"Could I go?"

"People would wonder why you're seein' her."

"So how do we find out how she is?" Zee asked.

"We'll just have to wait until we hear from her."

"Why would we hear from her?"

Jesse didn't answer.

"Jesse," Zee said, "did you try to recruit her? Are you trying to put a gang together?"

"Zee, I couldn't very well pass up a chance to have Lady Gunsmith in a gang, could I?"

"So you're telling me you only want to put together a gang because Roxy Doyle is in town?"

"Well . . ."

"No, you've been thinking about it. That's why you keep meeting with Bob Ford. Why not Charley? I'll tell you why," she went on, cutting him off before he could offer an answer. "You been plannin' all along, haven't you? You and Frank?"

"Look, Zee—"

"Never mind," she said. "Did it even occur to you that Roxy's been shot so you can't recruit her?"

"You're sayin' she was shot by somebody who knows that Thomas Howard is Jesse James?"

"And they know you're forming a new gang," she added. "Who have you been telling?"

He thought about that question. He had been very careful about who he told—Bob and Charley Ford, and Roxy Doyle. That was all.

"The Fords," he said. "Maybe they think they're helpin' me by killin' her."

"Maybe they're just jealous," Zee said. "I don't like them, Jesse. Especially that Bob. He's a little weasel."

"Charley's okay," Jesse insisted. "He rode with us before."

"But Bob's new," Zee reminded him.

"Yeah, he is," Jesse said, "but Charley vouched for him."

"Then you've told somebody else," she said, "and you don't remember who."

"No, I haven't," he insisted, "but I did send a telegram to Frank."

"The telegraph operator?"

"He's just a bored little man," Jesse said. "I can't see him with a gun, shootin' Roxy Doyle in the back."

"Maybe," Zee offered, "he's tryin' to impress you."

"Or maybe he talked to somebody else," Jesse added. "Crap! I'll have to go and see him."

"Go in the morning," Zee said. "Get a good night's sleep. Maybe somethin' will occur to you when you're rested."

He took off his jacket, hung it on the wall where a picture hung crookedly. He straightened it. He was always straightening it. What did it matter? A crooked picture wasn't going to kill him.

Chapter Thirteen

"Are you sure we can do this?" Mike Bowen asked.

"As long as you're gentle with me," Roxy said, "and don't open my wound again."

They had finished their meal, set aside the bowls and tray, and when she kissed him, he was eager—but then drew back and asked his question.

She began to unbutton his shirt, slid her hands inside to rub his hairless chest.

"Oh, I like this," she said. "No hair."

"Not one," he said.

"All over?" she asked.

"Well, there are some places—"

She slid a hand down between his legs, felt his hard penis through his trousers.

"Let me see," she said.

He stood up, undid his trousers and dropped them to the floor. His hard cock was impressive, as it jutted out of a forest of dark pubic hair.

"Very nice," she said, standing. She took his penis in her hand and stroked it, enjoying the feel of the smooth skin. Then she went to her knees.

"Roxy—" he said.

"I'm fine," she said. "I'm just going to . . . explore."

She took his penis in both hands, leaned in and slid it between her lips. She took as much of it into her mouth as she could, and then began rocking her head back and forth. He gasped, reached down to touch her hair. She kept sucking him until she had him good and wet, until he was standing on his toes, almost ready to finish, and then she released him.

"Get the rest of your clothes off," she said, urgently, as she started to remove her own.

When they were both naked, she got on the bed, careful of her bandaged shoulder.

"Come on, come on," she said, "I want that raging monster in me."

"But . . . your wounds."

"Keeps me from lying on my back so you can pound me," she said. "Also keeps me from bouncing up and down on you like I want to. But it doesn't keep us from doing this."

She got on her hands and knees and hiked her naked butt up. Just looking at her got him even more excited.

"Well, come on," she said, impatiently.

He got on the bed behind her and, misunderstanding her intention, started to spread the cheeks of her butt.

"No, not there," she said. "I'm good and wet. Just slide it up between my thighs and let's get going."

He did as she asked, slid his hard cock between her thighs and up into her wet vagina. He started to move in and out of her, holding her hips on either side.

"Let me know if I hurt you," he told her.

"Believe me," she said, "you'll be the first to know . . ."

***

They rocked together on the bed for some time and, as fast and hard as he got going, he never did manage to hurt her . . . much.

After he had exploded into her, he collapsed onto his back. She laid alongside him, with her head in the crook of his arm. Her right arm was between them, as she kept her left shoulder up so as not to put too much pressure on it. The door was locked—she'd had him jam the chair into place—and she felt sure that, if the need arose, she could still roll and grab her gun in a split second.

But for now, she rubbed her hand over that smooth chest, kissed his shoulder.

"That was good," she said.

"It sure was!" he agreed, enthusiastically. "It'll be even better when you're all healed."

She didn't respond to that. She knew that by the time she was healed, she'd be gone from this place. This coupling would probably never take place again, but for the moment it had been very satisfactory.

"Mike?"

"Yes?"

"Do you know for sure that your Captain Kelly talked to all the men about my father?"

"Oh, yeah," he said. "I saw him do most of it."

"And nobody knows anything?"

"I'm sorry, Roxy," he said, "but some of our younger men never even heard of your father. They've heard of you, of course, but not your father."

"But you have?" she asked. "You heard of Gavin Doyle?"

He hesitated, then said, "Actually, no, I never did. Sorry."

"That's all right," she said. "I guess he made his bones a lot of years ago."

"And you've been looking for him for years?"

"Uh, yes."

"How do you even know he's still alive?"

"I've followed up a lot of the rumors," she said. "I may not have found him, but I learned enough to know that he's still alive."

"So where do you go from here?"

"I don't rightly know," she said. "I guess I'll decide that when I'm done here."

"But what about—"

She rolled away from him.

"No more questions," she said. "I'm tired. I think you should go."

"Oh," he said, looking like a kicked puppy. "I thought I'd stay—"

"No," she said, "I prefer to sleep alone. I'll see you tomorrow."

He sat up. "All right."

She watched him dress, and then stand there awkwardly.

"So . . . tomorrow?" he asked.

"Yes," she said, "I'll be around tomorrow. I'll come by and see you. I should probably talk to your chief before I decide my next move."

He nodded, said, "Well, good night, then," and left.

She rose, replaced the chair beneath the doorknob, then went back to the bed and to sleep.

Chapter Fourteen

She rose in the morning, feeling stiff. Moving around the room a bit helped, and then she washed and got dressed. She decided to follow the doctor's orders, go by his office so he could change the bandage.

***

"There you go," he said. "Clean as a whistle."

She stood up, flexed her hands and arm.

"How does it feel?" he asked.

"Fine."

"Just don't do anything too strenuous," he said. "I don't want you to start that wound bleeding again."

"I'll be careful," she promised. "The most strenuous thing I'll do is lift a beer."

"Sounds good."

"But right now, I'm going to get some breakfast."

"Really?" he said. "Do you mind if I join you? I know a great little place, right around the corner."

"Sure," she said, "let's go."

She had the feeling the doctor had something he wanted to get off his chest. She just hoped the older gent wasn't interested in her for the usual male reasons.

***

They got seated at a table for two against the back wall of the small café Doc Willoughby took her to. They both got ham-and-eggs and started to work on their plates.

"Okay, Doc," she said. "What's this about?"

"Sorry?"

"You've got something on your mind," Roxy said. "Something you want to talk to me about."

"Yes, you're right," he said. "There is something. But first I had to be sure you were who you say you are."

"And?"

"Well," he said, "somebody tried to kill you. That's good enough for me."

"So then . . .what is it?"

"Your father."

"What about him?"

"He was here."

"Here? In St. Joe?"

He nodded.

"When?"

"Several weeks ago."

"Then why does no one remember him?"

"Because nobody saw him, but me."

"And how did that happen?" she asked.

"He'd been shot, needed a doctor. He came in one night, knocked on my door."

"And you let him in?"

"That's what I do," he said. "I treat injured and sick people. I opened the door and he fell into my arms. He'd been shot twice, once in the side, and then in the shoulder." He touched his own shoulder.

"From the back?"

"No, from the front."

"Who shot him? Why?"

"He wouldn't tell me that," Willoughby said, "and I didn't need to know in order to treat him."

"And I assume he pulled through?"

"I removed the bullets, bandaged him and after a few days, he left."

"And he still didn't tell you who or why?"

"No, he didn't."

"Was he shot in town?" she asked. "Could it have been the same one who shot me?"

"No, that much I do know," Willoughby said. "He rode in already injured."

"Well," Roxy said, "I appreciate you telling me this, Doc."

"Of course," he said. "I thought you had a right to know."

"Is there anything else?"

"Like what?"

"Like where he went when he left here?"

"No," Doc Willoughby said, "he just said he had some unfinished business."

"With the people who shot him."

"People?"

"Well," she said, "I assume it would have taken more than one to shoot him from the front. Tell me, the bullets you took out of him . . . they were from different guns, right?"

"That's very good," he said. "Yes, you're quite right. He was shot by two different people."

"And he left here to find them," she said. "That was his unfinished business."

"No doubt."

They finished their breakfast, and the doctor insisted on paying. She didn't object, since her funds were so low.

Outside he asked, "What will you do now? Still try to find him?"

"Yes," she said, "but not yet."

"Why not?"

"Because," she said, "I've got some unfinished business of my own around here."

Chapter Fifteen

When Roxy and Doc Willoughby went their separate ways, she walked directly to the police station. Mike Bowen looked up from the front desk as she entered, and he smiled.

"Good-morning," he said.

"'morning," she greeted. "How are you?"

"I'm great," he said. "How are you feeling?"

"Kind of sore," she said, "in places."

He blushed.

"I meant my shoulder," she added.

"Oh, yeah."

"Is your chief back, yet?"

"Uh, no. When we said he wasn't here, what we meant was he's out of town."

"So who's in charge? Captain Kelly?"

"That's right. Do you want to see him?"

"He's already been no help," she said. "What about Detective Nelson. Is he around?"

"Oh, yeah, he's here. Wait. I'll get him."

He left the desk, disappeared into the building, and then reappeared with Detective Nelson in tow.

"Miss Doyle," he said. "Glad to see you out and about."

"Detective. Can we talk?"

"Of course," he said. "Come with me. Thanks, Mike."

"Sure, Detective."

She followed him back into the building, but instead of taking her to an office, he simply took her to a desk.

"They said they were going to give me an office, but so far this is it. Have a seat."

She sat next to the desk while he sat behind it.

"I'm sorry, but I don't have anything to tell you yet about the shooting."

"And I don't have anything to tell you," she said, "except that I'm going to start looking, today. Asking questions."

"I see."

"I wanted to let you know that."

"Well, thank you."

"I'd better get to it."

She stood, then stopped.

"Detective, can I ask you something?"

"Sure, ask away," he said, leaning back in his chair and looking up at her.

"Have you ever heard of Gavin Doyle?"

"The bounty hunter? Sure. He's your father, right?"

"That's right. Some of your younger officers—like Mike, on the desk—have never heard of him. But you and Captain Kelly, you have."

"Right."

"If he came to St. Joe, would you recognize him?"

"That would be a no," Nelson said. "I've never seen him before."

"Right," she said. "Okay, well, thanks for talking to me, Detective."

"I'll walk you out," he said.

He walked her past the front desk and right to the front door, stepping outside with her.

"Miss Doyle."

"Yes?"

"Do you think your father was here?"

She decided not to share what Doc Willoughby had told her. If the sawbones wanted people to know what he'd done, he would have told them, by now.

"I don't know, Detective," she said. "But If I don't discover any indication of that by the time I find out who shot me, I'll be leaving."

"So you're not leaving until you find who shot you?" he asked.

"No, I'm not," she said.

Chapter Sixteen

After she left the police station, her next stop was Thomas Howard's house, on Lafayette Street. Looking at the situation realistically, the only person she knew of who might have a motive to kill her was Jesse James. He wouldn't want his identity revealed, and she was the only person who knew it, other than the people he trusted.

She walked to his house, looked around, made sure no one was watching, and only then approached the door and knocked. Zee opened it.

"Roxy!" Zee grabbed her hands and pulled her inside. "I'm so glad to see you on your feet. We heard you were shot."

"I was," Roxy said. "In the back of the shoulder."

"Somebody shot you from behind?"

"That's right."

"Coward! Do they know who it was?"

"Not yet," Roxy said. "But by God, I'm going to find out."

"Is that why you're here?" Zee asked. "To see if it was Jesse who shot you?"

"I don't mean to insult you, Zee, but—"

"Never mind that," Zee said. "I even asked him if he did it when he told me."

"He told you I was shot?"

"Yes. He heard it in town. Look, you better come in and sit down. You look pale."

"Is Jesse here?"

"He is. He's in the kitchen having a last cup of coffee."

Roxy followed Zee through the house to the kitchen, where Thomas Howard was sitting at the table with a cup.

"Roxy!" he said. "Damn, I'm glad you're up. How bad was it?"

"Back of the shoulder," she said. "Doc Willoughby said the bullet didn't hit anything vital."

"That's good to hear. Sit down."

He held a chair out for her, and she sat.

"Coffee?" Zee asked.

"Sure, thanks."

As Zee got her a cup of coffee, Jesse looked across the table at her.

"I know what you're thinkin'," he said. "Believe me, I didn't shoot you."

"I want to believe that, Jesse."

"I wouldn't have a reason to."

"To shut me up?"

"I don't want to shut you up," he said, "I want you to join me."

Roxy looked at Zee as she put a cup of coffee in front of her.

"Don't worry, Zee knows," Jesse said.

"I think I knew all along," Zee said, sitting down. "Jesse can't quit."

"So, you see?" Jesse said. "I need you alive."

"Okay," Roxy said, "then help me."

"How?" Jesse asked.

"Do you know anybody in town who might want to kill me?" Roxy asked. "Either for personal reasons, or just to get a reputation?"

"I'll have to give it some thought," he said.

"The Fords," Zee said.

Jesse gave her a look.

"I'm sorry, Jesse," she said. "I don't trust them like you do."

"Fords?" Roxy asked.

"Charley and Bob," Jesse said. "They're brothers. Charley rode with our original gang. Bob's his younger brother, and he's new."

"So you trust them, and Zee doesn't?"

"I trust Charley," Jesse said. "And he vouched for Bob."

"Can I talk to them?"

"Why?" he asked.

"If I'm going to join your gang, I've got to trust the other members," she said. "I have to feel sure that they didn't shoot me."

Jesse looked at Zee.

"She's right, Jesse."

"Yeah, I know she is," Jesse said. "All right, I'll set it up."

"There's one other thing," Roxy said.

"What's that?" Jesse asked.

"Do you know my father on sight?"

"Your father?"

"Gavin Doyle, the bounty hunter."

"No," he said, "luckily, Doyle's never been on my trail."

"Well, I found out he was here a few weeks ago," she said. "Doc Willoughby treated two bullet wounds."

"Somebody shot Doyle, too?" Jesse asked.

"Yes, but not here in St. Joe. He arrived already wounded, looking for a doctor."

"Did Willoughby tell anyone?"

"No, he kept it to himself," Roxy said. "But he told me this morning."

"Jesus," Jesse said. "Does Willoughby know where he was going when he left here?"

"No," she said, "just that he was looking for whoever shot him—and that's what I'm doing. I'm not leaving St. Joe until I find out who put this bullet hole in me."

"I don't blame you," Jesse said. "I'll get you together with the Fords later today."

"Leave me a message at my hotel," Roxy said. "I'm going to be asking questions around town. Somebody must've seen something, maybe a stranger in town."

She stood up, and Zee walked her to the front door.

"When you meet the Fords," she told Roxy, "push Bob. He's a weasel."

"Thanks, Zee," Roxy said. "I'll do that."

Chapter Seventeen

Roxy walked back to the part of town where she had been shot. There were stores in the area, so she stopped into them to ask if anyone had seen or heard anything around the time of the shooting the day before.

Several owners said no, they heard or saw nothing, but one—a woman who ran a hat shop—wasn't immediately forthcoming.

"Are you the gal who was shot, honey?" the middle-aged woman asked.

"Yes, Ma'am, I am."

"I assume it wasn't too bad?"

"I was shot in the back of the shoulder," Roxy said. "Doc Willoughby did a good job of patching me up."

"He's a good man," the woman said.

"Yes, he is."

"But I don't like these new policemen we got in town," the woman went on. "We had Sheriff Rhodes for a long time, but he's gone now."

"That's progress, I guess," Roxy said. "The police haven't been very helpful to me." She decided to play into the woman's irritation.

"They ain't helpful to nobody," the woman said, bitterly. "They've arrested my husband twice in the past few months, for no reason at all."

"That's a damn shame."

"So he drinks a bit," the woman went on, "gets a little rowdy. Sheriff Rhodes used to sober him up and send him home. These new police, they toss him in a cell and then send him home smellin' like jail."

"I sympathize, Ma'am," Roxy said, "and I'll leave you alone, now, to get your work done."

She turned to leave, hoping the woman would stop her.

"Well," the woman said, "I do have somethin' to tell you, but I don't know how helpful it'll be."

Roxy turned back.

"Whatever you can tell me, Ma'am, it'll be more than I have now."

"I saw somebody," the woman said, "seemed to be sneakin' around across the street, with a rifle."

"Sneaking?"

"Looked like they was tryin' not to be seen, ya know?" the woman asked.

"Did you recognize who it was?" Roxy asked.

"No," the woman said, "they had a bandana across their face, and a big hat pulled down."

"Was it a big man, small man?"

"Small," the woman said, "not big at all."

"And where did he go?"

"There's a storefront across the way that's vacant," the woman said. "I saw him sneakin' around there."

"Thank you, Ma'am," Roxy said, "that's very helpful. I appreciate it."

"Well, I hope you find whoever it was," the woman said. "It's a cowardly thing, shootin' somebody in the back."

"Yes, it is," Roxy said. "Thanks, again."

Roxy left the hat shop, crossed the street and found the vacant store.

The windows were boarded up, but the front door looked like the boards had been pried loose, just enough for a smallish person to squeeze in. Roxy needed to loosen a couple more before she could get inside.

With the windows boarded over, it was dark. It didn't look like a place somebody could take a shot from, but then Roxy saw some light coming from the ceiling. She walked to it, saw that there was a hatch in the ceiling, probably leading to the roof. A shot could certainly have been taken from up there.

She looked around, found a wooden crate big enough to offer access to the hatch. The only problem was she couldn't pull the carton over with just one hand, and even if she did, she couldn't climb up there with her shoulder wound inhibiting her. She needed help, and she thought she knew just the man to help her.

***

She went to the police station, found Mike Bowen behind the desk.

"You're back," Bowen said. "You want to see the detective again?"

"No," she said, "I'm here to see you."

"That's good," he said, "because I'm about finished here. If you want to wait—"

"Mike, I'm here to ask for your help," she said, cutting him off. "Not, you know, about last night."

"Oh, well, that's okay," he said. "Let me change clothes and I'll meet you out front."

"Don't wear anything too clean," she said. "The help I need is probably going to get you pretty dirty."

"Thanks for telling me," he said. "I won't wear my Sunday suit."

As another officer came out and replaced Bowen at the desk, Roxy went out front of the building to wait.

Chapter Eighteen

"Up there?" Bowen asked, looking up.

"Yes."

"What about in here?"

There was more light inside, because Bowen had to clear all the boards away from the door to get in. Once inside, he also pulled some boards away from the windows.

"Well, there's plenty of light here now, and we can see some footprints," Roxy said. "Also, these drag marks show that the crate was pulled over here, and then dragged back."

"You sure you're not a detective?" he asked.

"Well," she said, "the Pinkertons have tried to recruit me."

"Really? That's impressive."

"I turned them down."

"That's even more impressive," he said.

"Anyway," Roxy said, "we need to get a look at the roof."

"Let's do it, then," he said and dragged the crate over. Once he had it beneath the hatch, he stood up on it, reached up, slid the hatch aside, and then climbed up.

"Okay?" she called out.

"Fine. I'll walk around and take a look." He stuck his head back down through the hatch. "What am I looking for?"

"Anything," she said. "Footprints, a spent cartridge, a cigarette . . ."

"Okay, okay, I got it," he said, and withdrew his head.

She wished she could have had him reach down and pull her up onto the roof, but that would've definitely torn her stitches.

She could hear Bowen moving around on the roof, side-to-side, to the front, and even to the back, although that wasn't really necessary.

"I'm coming back down," he called.

She moved away from the crate just in case he slipped. She didn't want that big body falling on her.

His feet came through the hatch, felt for the crate, found it, and then he dropped down.

"What'd you see?"

"There's signs that somebody was up there, but they didn't leave anything behind but some footprints."

"Small?"

"Pretty small, yeah," Bowen said. "The man who shot you wasn't a big fella, that's for sure."

That left Jesse James out. She was glad. Of course, Jesse could have sent someone to do the job, but after talking to him and Zee, she didn't think that was the case.

He slapped his hands together to get some of the rooftop dirt off them.

"A small man who wants to kill me so much he'd shoot me in the back," she said. "Does that mean anything to you?"

"No," he said. "I've got to say, we don't have many killers in St. Joe. This is not the Wild West, you know."

"There are killers everywhere, Mike," Roxy said.

"I'd hate to think that," he said.

She thought he was terribly naïve for a lawman, but then he was very young.

"Well, thank you for your help."

"Is there anything else I can do for you?" he asked. "I'm free tonight. If you want to have supper—"

"I've got things to do, Mike," she said, "and I've already arranged to have supper with somebody."

"Oh," he said, looking disappointed. "Well, all right then."

They left the boarded-up building, and Bowen said, "Maybe I should put these boards back up."

"You'd need nails and a hammer," Roxy said. "You'll have to go and get them."

"I've got nothing else to do," he said. "So maybe I'll do just that."

"I'm sorry, Mike," she said. "I have to go."

She left him standing there, looking crestfallen.

***

Roxy wondered if either Charley or Bob Ford were small men. She figured to find out the answer to that question later that evening, if Jesse kept his word about introducing her.

When she got back to her hotel, the desk clerk came running out from behind the desk.

"A message came in for you, Miss Doyle," he said. He handed it to her.

"Did you see who brought it in?" she asked.

"No," he said, "I just found it on the desk when I came back from a break."

"All right, thank you."

"Of course," the young man said. "Anything else I can do—"

"No, no," she said, "this is fine."

He nodded and went back to his desk.

Roxy waited until she was in her room before unfolding the note. It was from Jesse and it said: MEET ME AT NINE AT THE BROKEN BRANCH SALOON.

She assumed he'd have the Fords with him. If she hadn't already decided she trusted him, she might worry that this could be a trap.

Chapter Nineteen

When Roxy got to the Broken Branch Saloon, she found it pretty busy for a small place. That was probably why Jesse had chosen it for the meeting. The problem was, Roxy stood out in any saloon, no matter how crowded they were. Men stopped what they were doing to watch her as she walked to the bar.

"Beer," she said.

The bartender looked at her and said, "You're askin' for trouble comin' here, girlie."

"I'm asking for a beer," she said, "you're the one asking for trouble if you don't give it to me."

The man stared at her for a few seconds, then drew her a beer and set it down in front of her.

"Four bits," he said.

"Wha—four bits?" she asked.

"The lady's beer is on me," a man said, coming up next to her.

"That's not nec—"

"Okay, Charley," the barman said, "if she's with you, two bits."

"Charley?" she said to the man. "As in Charley Ford?"

"That's right," the man said. "Why don't you pick up your beer and come with me?"

As he walked away, she did so, following him.

He led her through the crowded saloon to a table where another, smaller man sat.

"Roxy Doyle, this is my brother, Bob Ford," Charley said.

Bob looked up at her, but did not rise. Physically, she could see why Zee described him as a weasel, but she suspected Jesse's wife was talking about more than just his appearance.

"Have a seat," Bob Ford said.

Neither of the brothers were sitting with their back to the wall, so she took that chair.

"So Mr. Howard," Charley said, coming down very hard on the name, "said you wanted to meet us."

"You're thinkin' about joinin' us?" Bob asked.

"I'm considering joining Mr. Howard," she said, using the same inflection. "He invited me and I'm still thinking about it."

Charley and Bob exchanged a glance.

"Don't—" Charley started, but Bob beat him to it.

"We don't think we need you," he said.

"My brother is speaking for himself," Charley was quick to add.

"Fine," Bob said, "*I* don't think we need you. We'll do just fine without a woman in the gang."

"Is that your only objection?" she asked. "I'm a woman?"

"My brother's jealous of how much respect Mr. Howard seems to have for you."

"I ain't jealous!" Bob snapped. "I just think a woman in a gang means trouble."

"Correct me if I'm wrong," Roxy said, "but this would be your first gang, right?"

Charley, who was in his early thirties, laughed at his younger brother and said, "She's got you there, Bob."

"Damn you, Charley—" Bob hissed.

"Look, fellas," Roxy said, "even if I join this gang, I don't plan to be here long. On the other hand, you two will probably be following Mr. Howard for a long time."

"Just 'til we get our own gang," Bob said.

"You're right, Miss Doyle," Charley said. "There's no reason for us to resist having you in the gang. And I keep tellin' my brother that."

Bob took solace in his beer.

"Well, now that we've got that settled," she said, "which one of you shot me yesterday?"

Bob choked on his beer as Charley said, "What?"

"Come on," she said, "somebody put a bullet in my shoulder, and who else could it have been? I mean, who else knows that Mr. Howard recruited me?"

"Now wait a minute," Charley said. "Neither one of us took a shot at you. Why would we do that?"

"Well, you gave one reason, Charley," she said. "Jealousy."

"So you're sayin' it was me?" Bob asked. "I would never shoot nobody in the back!"

"The footprints I found at the scene indicate the shooter was a smaller man," she said. "How tall are you, Bob?"

"You can't pin this on me," Bob Ford said. "Jesse—Mr. Howard would be so mad at me if I shot you. I don't need that, believe me."

"Miss Doyle," Charley said, "my brother would never even think about that, believe me." He leaned in and lowered his voice. "He doesn't have the guts."

"Charley!" Bob snapped. "I do too!"

"Come on, Bob," Charley said, "you want her to think you did it? Really?"

Bob Ford looked into his beer again, then said, "Yeah, okay, fine. I don't have the guts."

"See?" Charley said.

"Okay," Roxy said, "so it wasn't either of you. Do you know anyone else in town who might've shot me? Somebody lookin' for a reputation."

"In this town?" Bob asked. "Why do you think Mr. Howard chose to settle here? Nobody in this town has any guts."

"Again," Charley said, "my brother's opinion."

"Why can't you ever back me up?" Bob demanded.

"Say somethin' that makes sense, just once," Charley said, "and I'll back you."

Roxy sipped her beer and then pushed it away and stood up.

"I think we're done here."

"So, what've you decided?" Charley asked. "Are you gonna join?"

"I haven't made my mind up about that, yet," she said. "I still have to give it some thought."

"See?" Bob said to his brother. "That's why we don't need a woman. They can never make up their minds."

"Shut up, Bob!" Charley snapped. "What about whoever shot you? Are you convinced it wasn't one of us?"

She studied the two brothers.

"I tell you what, Charley," she said, then. "I'm convinced it wasn't you."

"What about me?" Bob Ford asked.

She gave him a hard look.

"You know how we women are, Bob," she said. "I just haven't made my mind up, yet."

Chapter Twenty

Roxy was not convinced about the Ford brothers.

She suspected that Charley didn't shoot her, but also suspected that Zee was right about Bob—he was a weasel. And as such, maybe he had decided to keep Roxy out of the gang by killing her.

But if Charley was right, and Bob didn't have the guts, then she was back where she started.

Who shot her?

It was clear she was looking for a coward, someone who would go up on a rooftop and wait to bushwhack her. But she was in a town she had never been in before, and hadn't seen anyone other than Jesse who she knew. It was a "civilized" town with an honored history that included the Pony Express, not the Wild West.

And the town did have one thing that most Western towns had—bartenders. And she learned long ago that bartenders knew most of the people in town. However, bartenders came in all sizes, shapes, colors, and attitudes. For instance, the barman in the Broken Branch who had called her "girlie" would be no help to her, at all. She had already used some bartenders in her search for her father, so she decided to go back to the Horseshoe Saloon and see what she could find out.

***

As she entered the Horseshoe, she ignored the clientele and walked directly to the bar. She knew they were staring at her, some because of how she looked, some because of who she was, and some because they had heard she'd been shot.

The bartender remembered her and actually gave her a smile.

"Still looking for your father?" he asked.

"Not at the moment," she said to him. "Right now I'm looking for the yahoo who shot me in the back."

"I heard about that," he said. "It's nice to see you up on your feet."

"I'd never find the culprit lying on my back," she said. "I already know that he was up on a rooftop with a rifle, waiting for me."

"Coward," the bartender said.

"You've got that right," she said. "And he was a small man. Does this sound familiar to you, at all?"

"A small coward with a rifle?" he asked. "Let me think about that."

"You hear all the conversations in here," Roxy said to him. "You know these men. They're your customers."

"And that means I'm not lookin' to throw anybody to the wolves," he said. "Or to you."

"I understand that, believe me," she said. "But I swear I'm not looking to kill anybody. What I'm looking for is the reason he shot me. Does it have something to do with who I am? Or does it have something to do with my father?"

"I get it, Miss Doyle."

"Just call me Roxy."

"Okay, Roxy."

"And you're Artie, right?"

"You remembered."

"Artie, I'm not asking you to give up a friend," she said. "I'm just asking you for your best guess."

"You know," he said, "I've worked in saloons in the West where the answer would've been every other man in the place. This is a lot harder."

"I appreciate that," she said.

"Come and see me tomorrow," he said, "and I'll try to have an answer for you."

"Okay," she said, finishing her beer. "I'll be back tomorrow."

Chapter Twenty-One

Roxy decided that talking to the one bartender was enough. The Horseshoe was the biggest saloon in town, so Artie would be the busiest bartender. She went back to her room. In the morning she intended to once again check in at the police department, this time with Detective Nelson to see what he knew about the Ford brothers. She just needed to think of a reason she'd be asking that question, one that had nothing to do with Jesse "Thomas Howard" James.

***

The Ford boys remained in the saloon after Roxy left, and continued to drink.

"Did you have to do that?" Bob demanded.

"Do what?"

"Humiliate me in front of that woman."

"That woman happens to be our chance to be part of a legendary gang," Charley said. "If she and Jesse work together, there's no tellin' what we could do."

"You're crazy!" Bob said. "Her and Jesse? They'll kill each other."

"Why do you say that?"

"Can't you see it?" Bob asked. "They'll both want to lead the gang. It'll come down to him or her."

"You're crazy," Charley said. "Nobody's gonna challenge Jesse James, not even Lady Gunsmith."

"Why do you think Jesse is God?" Bob asked.

"I rode with him, Bob," Charley said. "I saw what he can do."

"And what's that?'

"Anythin' he wants!" Charley stood up. "I'm goin' back to the hotel. You comin'?"

"I'll be along later."

"Don't drink too much more," Charley warned. "You know what happens when you get drunk."

"Yeah, yeah . . ."

Bob Ford watched his brother leave the saloon, then poured himself another drink from the bottle they'd been sharing. He was going to have to put his plan into action, and soon. All he needed was to hear when from the Governor. And he was going to have to make sure Charley didn't turn on him when the time came.

***

Zee came into the living room and looked at Jesse, seated on the couch, brooding.

"Are you coming to bed, Mr. Howard?"

"Soon, Mrs. Howard," he said.

She walked over and sat beside him. He put his arm around her and drew her close.

"What's bothering you?" she asked.

"I haven't heard from Frank in a while," he said.

"You will," she said. "He never stays out of touch for very long."

"I need to tell him about Roxy," he said. "Once he knows she's joining us, I know he'll be in."

"And you're still determined to use the Fords?"

"The gang can't very well be Frank, Roxy and me," he said. "We need more."

"Yes, but them?"

"Why are you so dead set against them, Zee?"

"It's not so much Charley," she said. "It's just that . . . Bob!"

"What's he ever done to you?" Jesse asked. Then he looked at her. "Did he ever try anything with—"

"No, no, it's not that," Zee said. "He's never touched me. It's the way he . . . looks."

"The way he looks at you? At me?"

"It's the way he *looks*," she said again, this time pointing to her face.

Jesse laughed.

"You don't like his looks?"

"I'm warning you, Jesse," she said. "He's a weasel."

"I know," Jesse said. "You keep sayin' that, but I never thought you meant he actually looks like a weasel."

"Why don't you try somebody else?"

"Because everybody else is either dead or in jail," he said. "The Youngers are in prison, Wood Hite's dead, Chapman and Bugler are in jail . . . there's nobody left."

"Then find some new blood," she said.

"I'd have to come out from behind Thomas Howard to do that," he said. "No, I'll stick with Bob and Charley. And with Frank and Roxy, we'll have an unbeatable gang."

Zee leaned in and kissed her husband's cheek.

"I hope you're right." She stood up. "I'm going to bed."

"I'll be along," he said.

He remained on the sofa for some time after Zee went to sleep, thinking about the Fords, about Frank, and about Roxy Doyle. Lady Gunsmith hadn't given her final decision yet. Tomorrow, he would press her for it. It was possible he was going to have to help her find out who shot her before she'd join.

Chapter Twenty-Two

Roxy woke the next morning feeling stiff again. She got out of bed, moved around the room a while, flexing and stretching just enough to loosen up, not enough to tear her stitches. By the time she was washed and dressed, she didn't feel the need to go and see Doc Willoughby again.

She went downstairs for breakfast.

***

"You want me to what?" Zee asked, the next morning.

"Take Roxy a message," Jesse said. "I can't be seen talkin' to her—at least, not at her hotel, and not in the street."

"What do you want me to tell her?"

"Have her meet me later today at the Broken Branch Saloon. It's the place people are less likely to see us together, or even care."

"Yes, but does Thomas Howard want to be seen in the Broken Branch?" Zee asked.

"I've been there with Bob and Charley," he said. "Besides, I'll just meet her there, and then we'll go somewhere else."

"Why do you want to see her?" Zee asked. "When she makes up her mind, she'll let you know."

"I want to help her find out who shot her."

"How?" Zee asked. "How's Thomas Howard going to do that?"

"I don't know, but if I do, she's sure to join the gang," Jesse said. "Don't you see? She'll owe me."

"And that's how you want to get her? By making her owe you?"

"Any way I can, Zee," Jesse said. "We need 'er!"

Zee took a deep breath.

"All right, Jesse," she said. "But tell me exactly when you want to meet her . . ."

***

As Roxy came down to the lobby, she saw Zee James in the lobby, wearing a simple cotton dress, holding a drawstring purse and looking nervous.

"Zee? What are you doing here?"

"Can we walk?" Zee asked.

"Well, sure."

They left the hotel together.

"Aren't you afraid to be seen with me?" Roxy asked.

"Let's walk down to this dress shop I go to," she said. "It'll just look like we're shopping."

Roxy let Zee take her to the dress shop, and they stopped in front of the window.

"Oh, that's pretty," Zee said, about a dress on display.

"Zee," Roxy said, "we're not really here about dresses, are we?"

"No, we're not," Zee said. "Jesse wants to see you."

"About what?"

"I should let him tell you," Zee said, "but he wants to help you find out who shot you."

"I can use all the help I can get," Roxy said, "but does Thomas Howard want to be seen with me?"

"He wants to meet at the Broken Branch, and then go someplace more private."

"And when will that be?"

"At seven," Zee said. She turned and looked at Roxy. "Maybe you'll have found out the answer yourself by then."

"That'd be great," Roxy said. "Listen, I'm going to have breakfast now. Would you like to join me?"

"I'd love to," Zee said, "but the question is, should I?"

"We could talk about dresses," Roxy offered. "Besides, who's going to care?"

"You're right," Zee said. "And if we talk about dresses, maybe we can come back here and buy one."

"You can," Roxy said. "I'm very low on funds."

"In that case, breakfast will be on me," Zee said.

"No, I couldn't—"

"Look, I have no friends in this town, Jesse wants us to stay away from locals as much as possible. So that leaves you and me."

"Well, in that case, I accept."

"And I know just the place. Come on."

***

Zee led Roxy to a small café on a side street.

"I've eaten here before, but always alone," Zee said. "It's nice to have somebody to share it with."

"Jess—Thomas hasn't been here with you?"

"No, he's usually too busy."

"Doing what?"

"Let's sit down and we can talk," Zee said.

A waiter let them have a table in the back, as the place was half empty at the moment.

After they had ordered, Roxy asked again, "What does Thomas do all day?"

"I thought he was looking for some kind of work," Zee said. "Now, as it turns out, he was trying to put a new gang together."

"And so far?"

"So far he has the Fords and, he hopes, Frank."

"And me."

"Yes," Zee said, "you."

"I met with the Fords last night," Roxy said.

"And what did you think?"

"Charley seemed okay, but Bob . . . there was something . . ."

"Weasel-like?"

". . . about him, yes."

Zee lowered her voice. "I know, I keep warning Jesse about him, but he won't listen."

"Well, Bob seems dead set against me joining the gang," Roxy said. "Maybe Jesse won't like that."

"You'll have to tell him yourself when you meet tonight," Zee said.

The waiter brought their breakfasts, and they stopped talking while he set them down. When he left Zee picked up her fork.

"Why don't we eat breakfast," she suggested, "and talk about dresses. It'll give you a nice break."

"Why not?" Roxy asked, and picked up her fork.

Chapter Twenty-Three

Roxy's interest in dresses was extremely limited, but it seemed to her that it was Zee who needed the break. So she allowed her to keep talking about them, until they finished their breakfast.

"Zee," she said, then, "I have to go over to the police department and talk to a detective there."

"About who shot you?"

"Yes. He's trying to find out who it was."

"All right, then," Zee said. "I'll pay for breakfast, and then I guess I'll go back to the dress shop myself."

She paid and they went outside, stopping in front of the café.

"I suppose you don't have much use for dresses, do you?" Zee asked Roxy.

"No, I'm afraid not," Roxy said. "I spend too much time on horseback."

"Well," Zee said, "thank you for letting me prattle on, then."

"It was my pleasure," Roxy said. "Maybe it was a nice break for both of us."

"Yes, I think it was," Zee said. "When you see Thomas tonight, make sure you tell him how you felt when you met Bob Ford. Maybe he'll listen to you."

"I will."

For a moment Roxy thought Zee was going to hug her, but she probably thought better of doing it on the street.

"I'll be seeing you," Zee said instead, and headed back to the dress shop.

Roxy realized when Zee said she had no friends, she was really speaking for both of them, Zee and Roxy.

***

"Roxy," Mike Bowen said. "Hi."

"Hello, Mike."

"Detective Nelson, again?"

"I'm afraid so," she said. "I'm sorry I haven't had the time—"

"It's okay," Bowen said. "I understand. I'll take you back there."

"Before we go, did you tell him what we found on the roof of that building?"

"No," Bowen said. "I didn't think I should tell him that I helped you."

"That's good," she said. "I'll just say I found it."

"Okay, good."

Roxy followed Bowen back to Nelson's desk, where the detective was sitting, staring at something.

"Detective, it's Roxy Doyle again," Bowen said. "I thought I'd bring her right back—"

"That's okay, Bowen," Nelson said. "Thanks."

Bowen nodded, turned and headed back to his post.

"Have a seat, Miss Doyle."

Roxy sat next to Nelson's desk, as the detective seated himself.

"I still don't have anything for you, yet," he said. "I'm sorry."

"That's okay," she said. "I asked some questions myself in the area. Most of the people gave me the same answers you got, except for one."

"Oh? Who was that?"

Roxy told Nelson what the woman had told her about the small man she saw sneaking around. Then she told him about the abandoned building, and the footprints she had found. She didn't mention Bowen.

"How'd you get up on the roof?" he asked.

"Oh, there was a crate I used—I think the shooter used it, too."

"I'll go over there and take a look," Nelson said. "So, a smallish man with a rifle?"

"That's what she said."

"Well, it's more than I got. I'm impressed."

"Can I ask you something?"

"Sure, go ahead."

"Do you know two brothers named Ford?"

"Ford? No, never heard of them. Why?"

"I met them in a saloon," she said, "Charley and Bob Ford. Bob is the younger one, and he's a smallish man."

"So you think he might've been the one who shot you?" Nelson asked.

"I actually don't have any reason to suspect him," she said. "I was just wondering if you knew them."

"Sorry. I can talk to them, though, if you like. What saloon did you see them in?"

Suddenly, she didn't want to tell him about the Broken Branch. Not when she was going to meet Jesse there later.

"No, that's all right," she said, instead. "I don't want to cause them any unnecessary trouble." She stood up. "Thanks for seeing me."

"I'll keep looking," he promised.

"So will I," she said, and left.

Chapter Twenty-Four

One of the reasons Roxy had turned down Robert Pinkerton's invitation to join the Pinkertons was that she wasn't sure she had what it took to be a detective. (There was also the fact that she had no desire to be a strike-breaker.)

Now, as she was walking away from the police station, she was even more convinced of it, mainly because she couldn't think of her next move.

Having breakfast with Zee actually had been a nice break, but now she needed to get her head back where it belonged—finding out who shot her. She probably needed the help of somebody in town, and Jesse James was the only one she could think of. So it was a good thing he already wanted to meet with her.

But that wasn't going to happen until seven p.m. What could she do between now and then that would be productive?

And that was when she realized she would never be a detective, because a detective would know their next move.

She had already talked to Jesse and Zee, and the Fords. Nobody was left—and then she remembered Artie, the bartender at the Horseshoe. She was supposed to talk to him again today, to see if he had come up with anything—or rather, anybody.

And she figured now was as good a time as any.

***

The Horseshoe's front doors were open. When she entered, it was empty, except for Artie, behind the bar.

"Good mornin'," he said.

"Artie." She approached the bar. "Looks like you just opened."

"We get a few early drinkers," he said. "Some people like their beer and whiskey for breakfast."

"I'll take coffee, if you got it."

"Actually, I do. In the back. Belly up and I'll get it."

She bellied up to the bar and waited, and he soon returned with a mug of steaming coffee.

"Thanks," she said, accepting it. "I guess you know why I'm here."

"I was gonna have a guess for you," Artie said. "About that thing you asked me about."

"Right. A small man with big talk, maybe."

"Well," Artie said, "we get quite a few big talkers in here, as you can guess. They get drunk and spout off about big plans they never have when they're sober."

"Right."

"Like maybe killing Lady Gunsmith."

"Right again."

He leaned his elbows on the bar.

"I've given this a lot of thought."

"And?"

He straightened up.

"I haven't been able to come up with anything," he said, "or anybody. Sorry."

"No big plans?"

"Oh, sure," he said. "There's two guys who keep talkin' about robbin' the St. Joe Bank. They're never gonna do it, naturally. There's another fella keeps talkin' about leaving here and goin' to St. Louis. That ain't such a big thing, but he ain't never gonna do it."

"But nobody talks about wanting to be a legend?" she asked. "A gunfighter?"

"Folks around here sorta figure that's a thing of the past," Artie said. "St. Joe's got some big plans of its own, Miss Doyle. Havin' gunfights in the street ain't one of them."

"Well," she said, "somebody decided it might be worth it."

"It'd be my guess," Artie said, "that it weren't nobody local."

"I'll bet that's a good guess," she said. "Somebody brought an outsider in to do the job. But why?"

"Somebody don't want you doin' what you're doin'," Artie said. "So what're you doin'?"

"Right now," she said, "I'm just looking for my father. I got the word that he was here, and now he's gone."

"Wait a minute," he said. "Gavin Doyle was here? And he didn't come into the Horseshoe?" The bartender seemed insulted.

"He didn't do much," Roxy said. "He was here a day or two and left."

"So you gettin' back on his trail?"

"I am," she said. "As soon as I find out who shot me."

"So if they wanted to get rid of you," he said, "by shootin' you, they made sure you stayed."

"That's about the size of it."

He shook his head.

"Stupid move. If you're gonna shoot somebody, you gotta make sure they're dead."

"All right, well," she said, "thanks for the coffee, and the opinions. I guess I'll just get back out there and keep looking."

"You need somebody to watch your back," Artie said.

"You got any suggestions for that?"

He rubbed his jaw and said, "I just might."

Chapter Twenty-Five

There's always somebody in any town willing to do anything for money. Even a so-called civilized town like St. Joseph, Missouri. The only problem was that Roxy didn't have any money.

"Find a guy named Bob Wolfe," Artie told her. "He might take the job just because you're Lady Gunsmith."

"For free?"

"Wait until you meet Wolfe."

"Where does he live?"

"He spends a lot of time here in the evenings," Artie said, "but he has a cabin outside of town, about two miles north."

"Then I guess I'll check there, first," Roxy said. "Thanks for the suggestion."

"Any time," he said. "Just keep comin' back here to drink."

"That's a promise."

She left the saloon and headed for the livery to collect her new horse.

***

She rode two miles north and came to a cabin. From the outside it looked barely large enough to have one room.

Riding up to the front, she heard a familiar sound from behind the cabin. Someone was chopping wood.

She dismounted, tied the horse off and walked around. She saw a tall, bare-chested man swinging an axe to chop firewood. When he spotted her, he stopped and stared. They did that to each other for several seconds. Off to one side was a lean-to with two horses inside.

He looked to be in his thirties, tall, fit, black-haired and almost handsome. Only a once or twice broken nose kept it from being so.

"I didn't send for a woman," he said in a deep voice, "but you'll do."

"Are you Bob Wolfe?"

"I am."

"My name is Roxy Doyle."

He looked surprised.

"Why is Lady Gunsmith comin' to see me? And how did you know where I live?"

"The bartender at the Horseshoe told me."

"Artie," he said. "Good guy."

"Yes, he is."

Wolfe picked up his gunbelt, which was lying nearby, slung it over his shoulder, and then took up an armload of firewood.

"Come on inside," he said. "We'll talk over some coffee."

She followed him around to the front and inside. She'd been right. The cabin was all one room, with a bed, a table, a stove and a fireplace. He dropped the wood near the fireplace, then walked to the stove.

"So, coffee? Or somethin' stronger?"

"Coffee 'll do."

He poured coffee into a chipped mug and carried it to her.

"I heard you were beautiful," he said. "But I never would've expected this."

"Thank you."

"Have a seat."

She sat at the scarred wooden table while he poured himself a cup, and then joined her.

"What can I do for you, Miss Doyle?"

"I heard that your gun was for sale."

"I don't hire out to kill people."

"That's not what I want."

"Then what *do* you want me to do?"

"Watch my back."

"If what I heard was right, you already got shot in the back once."

"That's true, in the shoulder. Doc Willoughby patched me up. I'm trying to find out who shot me and why."

"Before they do it again."

"Yes."

"And you want me to keep it from happenin' again?" he asked.

"Yes."

"How much can you pay me?"

"Nothing."

He raised his eyebrows.

"That's quite an offer."

"One I don't expect you to accept," she said.

"Then why did you come?"

"Because I had to ask. I don't know anybody in town, and Artie suggested you might be interested."

"If and when you find out who shot you," he asked, "and who sent them, is there any chance I could get paid?"

"Probably not."

"Boy, you're not givin' me much to work with, are you?" he asked.

She put the coffee cup down, still full.

"Thanks for listening." She stood up.

"Now, now, don't be hasty," he said, waving at her to sit back down. "Drink your coffee. Let's talk."

She sat.

"What *can* you offer me?"

"Just the opportunity to back me up," she said.

"To back up the Lady Gunsmith."

"Yes."

"I see."

He sipped his coffee. She picked hers up and did the same. It was strong.

"Well," he said, looking around, "my firewood is chopped, and I have nothing else to do. When do we start?"

"Now," she said. "I still have to walk around town and ask some questions. I'll just need you to make sure nobody shoots me in the back—again."

"Just give me a chance to clean up and get dressed," he said.

He stood up, walked to an old chest of drawers and took out some clothes, then abruptly dropped his trousers. He wore nothing underneath. His buttocks were perfectly rounded and firm, and drew her eyes.

She figured she better leave before he turned around.

"I'll wait outside," she said.

"Up to you," he said, without turning.

She went outside and stood by her horse.

Chapter Twenty-Six

When Bob Wolfe came out, he was fully dressed in Levis and a checkered shirt, a black hat, and wearing his gun on his right hip.

"I'll saddle my horse."

"First," she said, "that tree over there has a small branch about halfway up, with no leaves on it."

"I see it."

"Can you hit it?"

"Is this my audition?" he asked.

"I just need to know who I'm trusting my back to," she told him.

"Can't blame you for that."

He drew quickly and fired. The branch she had pointed out went flying off the tree with one shot.

"Happy?" he asked, ejecting the spent shell and replacing it. But the shot and the immediate reload impressed her. As had his naked ass.

"Yes," she said.

"I'll saddle up."

He walked around behind the house, returned in minutes, walking his horse, a six or seven-year-old dun with a grey coat and black mane.

"Ready?"

"I'm ready," she said.

They mounted up and headed for St. Joe.

***

Upon arrival, they reined in their horses in front of the Horseshoe. Roxy realized she may have miscalculated. Having Wolfe watch her back was one thing, but she couldn't very well take him with her when she met Jesse James at the Broken Branch. She was going to have to figure out how to leave him behind, but still have him be willing to watch her back when she wanted him to.

"I'll want to put my horse back in the livery," she said.

Wolfe looked at the Horseshoe longingly, then said, "Fine. I'll ride there with you and board my horse, too."

She nodded, and they continued on.

The livery was the largest one in town, and the one she had bought her horse from. A question occurred to her to ask as they left their horses.

"Have you seen any other strangers in town since I arrived?" she asked the man.

"Not a one," he said, "but there are other livery stables in town."

"Can you tell me where they are?"

The hostler looked at Wolfe.

"I know where they are," Wolfe said. "I'll take you."

"Good," she said, "if we could find another stranger's horse, we might find our shooter."

"Unless he's local."

They stepped outside and started walking.

"Do you know anyone who would take that job?" she asked.

"The only local I know of who might even be offered the job is me."

"But you don't hire your gun out that way." Plus, he was much too big to fit the footprints she'd found in that abandoned storefront.

"That's right," he said, "so nobody tried. Then your thought that it might be a stranger is probably true."

They walked back toward the Horseshoe Saloon, with Wolfe choosing the destination.

"Let's get a drink before we start checking liveries," he suggested.

"Fine," she said.

They entered the Horseshoe, which had started doing a brisk business, already.

Artie smiled as Roxy and Wolfe approached the bar.

"So you found him," he said.

"I found him."

"And you made your deal?"

"Yeah," Wolfe said, "Sex for watchin' her back."

"What?"

"He took the job because his firewood was already chopped," Roxy pointed out.

"Oh," Artie said. He looked at Wolfe. "Smart ass."

"Beer?" Wolfe asked Roxy.

"Sure."

"Give the smart ass and the lady a beer," Wolfe said to Artie.

"Comin' up."

He set the mugs on the bar and looked at Roxy.

"So now that you've got somebody to watch your back, are you gonna walk around town with a target on your ass—'scuse me."

"Not exactly," she said, "but that might work."

"We're gonna check the livery stables, see if any strangers rode in during the last few days."

"Sounds like a good move."

"Any strangers in here of late?" Wolfe asked.

"Just this lady," Artie said. "But we usually get a few durin' the course of a week."

"Somebody riding in now wouldn't fit," Roxy said, "unless they're coming in to help the shooter finish the job."

Artie moved down the bar to serve other customers.

"Has it occurred to you that it was just somebody shooting because you *are* Lady Gunsmith?" Wolfe asked.

"I think I've considered every possibility," she said. "Somebody who doesn't want me to find my father, somebody who just wants to kill me because of who I am, mistaken identity—"

"Not much chance of that," he said. "There's nobody else who looks like you, believe me."

"—or somebody who's got plans in town."

"Plans?"

"Robbing the bank?"

"Only the James/Younger gang would try that, and they're not in business, anymore."

She didn't comment on that.

But then she asked, "Do you know Jesse James?"

"Never met him or saw him," Wolfe said. "Wouldn't know 'im if he walked up to me and smiled. Why?"

"Just wondering, since you mentioned him."

They finished their beers and Wolfe asked, "Another?"

"Let's check those stables first," she said. "We can come back later."

"Okay," he said, "you're the boss."

Chapter Twenty-Seven

There were half a dozen livery stables in St. Joe, coming in small, medium and large.

One hostler said the only stranger he'd had in the past few days came in on a buggy, driven by an older couple. Another had two riders come in together, but they were kids.

"Did they have guns?" Wolfe asked.

"A small caliber rifle between them," the man said. "More like a pea shooter, for hunting."

"Did they say why they were here?" Roxy asked.

"No, but my feeling is they ran away from home. The older one couldn't be more than fourteen."

Roxy and Wolfe left that livery.

"They'd fit the bill," Wolfe said. "Small."

"Why would a couple of kids want to kill me?" she asked.

"Maybe you killed their pa," Wolfe suggested.

"I haven't killed anybody in months," she said. "I don't even think they're worth checking out."

She now had an idea for how to get rid of Wolfe that evening so she could meet Jesse, without getting the man suspicious.

***

After they checked the other stables they went back to the Horseshoe for that second beer. The place had filled up, but Wolfe elbowed them room for two at the bar with no trouble. Men seemed to defer to him.

"You got any friends in town?" she asked him.

"Why do you ask?"

"Well, other than Artie, I haven't seen you exchange two words with anybody."

"I'm concentrating on coverin' your back," he said. "I don't have time for friends."

Roxy had the feeling that was his attitude toward friendship whether she was there, or not.

"So," he said, "Are you gonna at least buy me supper?"

"I would, Wolfe," she said, "but I've got no money."

"How are you gonna pay for your hotel?"

"I'm not sure," she said. "I guess I might have to wash some dishes."

"I doubt that," he said. "I can't see you in a kitchen."

"Isn't that where women belong?" she asked.

"Not when they look like you," he said.

"We can each buy our own," she told him.

"Well," he said, "you asked if I had any friends, so I'm gonna take you someplace we can eat for free."

"Free?"

"They owe me," he said. "Come on."

***

He took her to a small restaurant, and it turned out to be the one Zee had taken her to.

"I've eaten here," she said.

"Then you know the food's decent."

As they entered, the waiter said, "Bob, it's good to see you."

"Good to see you, too, Eddie. Can you feed the two of us. We're a little shy of cash."

"No problem," the waiter said. "Have a seat."

They took a table in the back.

"See?" Wolfe said. "You're already benefiting from hirin' me."

"I appreciate that."

"Although to be hired," he went on, "I think you have to be gettin' paid. So I guess what you did was recruit me."

"Maybe," she said, "I just asked you for a favor."

"Which I gave," he said, "like a gentleman."

"Yes, you did." For a moment the memory of him standing naked in the cabin came to her, but she forced it away.

When the waiter came back, it was with plates of food Roxy had not even heard Wolfe order. But everything was sumptuous and delicious, and for the next half hour they were too busy eating to talk very much.

Chapter Twenty-Eight

After they had eaten, Roxy still had a couple of hours before meeting Jesse at the Broken Branch. She and Wolfe spent it working the streets, talking to shop owners, seeing if anyone else saw a "smallish man" sneaking around. They came up empty, and then stopped into the Horseshoe for a third time. It was there Roxy played her hand.

"Wolfe," she said, "why don't you check on those kids who rode in and left their horses at that second livery we stopped in."

"And what are you gonna do?" he asked.

"I have a meeting with somebody who wanted to see me alone," she explained.

"You think that's smart?" he asked. "I mean, I don't want you gettin' shot my first day on the job."

"No, it's okay," she said. "I trust this . . . person I'm meeting. I won't be long. I can meet you back here at eight."

"You really want me to check on those kids, or are you just tryin' to get rid of me?" he asked.

"I really want you to check on them," she lied. "I don't want to find out the answer was under a stone we left unturned."

"Wow!' he said. "That's very poetic. Okay, I'll see you back here at eight. Be careful."

She wanted to say she was always careful, but, after all, somebody *had* shot her in the back.

***

She walked into the Broken Branch, hoping the Fords wouldn't be there, happy to see that they weren't. But neither was Jesse, so she went to the bar and ordered a beer.

"Back again?" the bartender asked, setting the beer down in front of her. "Are you lookin' for trouble?"

"What kind of trouble do you think I'm looking for?" she asked.

"You're too damn pretty to be in this place," he said. "These yahoos won't be able to control themselves around a woman like you after they've had a few."

"I'll take my chances," she said. "I think I can count on you to protect me."

"Don't bet on it," he said, and moved off down the bar.

Roxy drank her beer and watched the front doors. She wanted to know as soon as "Thomas Howard" walked in, and then hustle him out of there.

***

Howard/Jesse didn't show.

Roxy had two beers, checked the time, and wondered what the hell was going on. She never would have arranged to meet Jesse out in the open. It was he who asked her to meet him. And now he wasn't there.

She had no choice but to go to his house and see what the hell was happening?

***

She knocked on the door of the Howard house and waited. When no one answered, she started to worry that maybe Jesse and Zee were inside, and either hurt or in trouble. After eating a meal with Zee and talking to her for a good length of time, she liked the woman, and didn't want to think she might be hurt. So she felt justified breaking into their home.

She tried to force the front door, but it was solid. She wasn't yet ready to break a window, so she walked around to the back of the house. The door, which led to the kitchen, was not as firm. It yielded to her shoulder, and she entered. As she did, she thought she heard someone crying. She walked through the kitchen to the living room and there she saw Zee James on the floor, holding Jesse's bloody head in her lap.

"Zee?" she said.

Zee looked up at her, her face streaked with tears.

"He's dead, Roxy," she said. "Jesse's dead."

"What the hell happened?" Roxy asked, shocked.

"He shot him."

"Who did?"

"That weasel, Bob Ford," Zee said. "He shot Jesse in the back of the head while he was cleaning off a picture on the wall." She shook her head. "I always told him to leave the damn picture alone. He was always cleaning or straightening it. And now . . ."

Roxy walked to Zee and bent over her. Jesse was pale and bloody.

"When did this happen?"

"I—I don't know," Zee said. "I don't know how long I've been sitting here holding him. Charley and Bob came over to talk to Jesse about you—or so they said. I went in the kitchen to make coffee, and the next thing I knew I heard the shot. I ran in, saw Jesse on the floor, and Bob Ford with a gun in his hand. Charley looked shocked, but then they both ran out of the house."

"So you haven't sent for the law?"

"Roxy, I haven't done anything but sit here and hold Jesse. I think I was expecting him to open his eyes and laugh at me."

"Zee . . . just stay where you are, all right? I'm going to get the law."

"But . . . we'll have to tell them who Jesse is," Zee said.

"What does it matter now?" Roxy said. "He's dead."

"I—I suppose you're right."

"I'll be back as soon as I can."

It was dusk when Roxy left 1318 Lafayette Street, April 3rd, 1892.

Chapter Twenty-Nine

When Roxy walked into the police station, she didn't expect to see Bowen still at the front desk, but it was just as well he was. She didn't have to identify herself and convince another officer that she was serious. She told Bowen what had happened and his eyes widened.

"Holy shit" he said. "Wait here."

He went and got Kelly, who came out with two other officers and asked Roxy, "Are you sure about this?"

"Sure that he's dead, or sure he's Jesse James?" she asked. Before Kelly could answer she said, "The answer to both is yes."

"Then let's go . . ."

Roxy led them to Jesse's house, although Kelly did stop at Doc Willoughby's office first to collect the doctor. They all went in the back door and found Zee right where Roxy had left her, with her husband's head in her lap.

"Ma'am," Captain Kelly said, "let me help you up so the doctor can have a look."

He almost lifted Zee completely off her feet and set her on the sofa. Doc Willoughby crouched down beside the body and rolled the man over.

"I know this man," he said. "It's Thomas Howard."

"His real name," Zee said, "is Jesse James."

"My God!" Willoughby said.

"Is he dead, Doc?" Kelly asked.

"Oh yeah, he's dead."

"Ma'am?" Kelly said to Zee. "What's your name?"

"Zerelda James," she said. "I'm Jesse's wife."

"You two," Kelly said to the officers he had brought with him, "go out front. When this gets around, people are gonna flock here."

"They already are," Bowen said, looking out the front window. "There's folks with torches."

"Torches?" Zee said. "Are they going to burn down my house?"

"I think they're just using them for light," Bowen said to her. "It's gotten dark out."

"All right," Kelly said. "I'm going to talk to them, and then I'll be back in and my officers will keep them out. Bowen, you cover the back door. I don't want any newspaper people to bother this woman."

"Yes, sir."

"Miss Doyle," Kelly said. "Will you stay with Mrs. James?"

"Of course I will," Roxy said. She sat down next to Zee, who was shaking, and put her arms around her.

"I'll be back" Kelly said, and went outside with his officers."

"Ma'am," Willoughby said, "I'll have some men come and take him to the undertaker's office."

"Yes, yes, all right," Zee said. Turning to Roxy she asked, "What about Bob Ford?"

"When the Captain comes back we'll tell him, and he'll have Ford picked up."

"If he hasn't left town," Zee said. "I told Jesse. I told him to watch out for Ford."

"He should've listened," Roxy said.

"Damn right he should've listened," she said. "Oh my God, I have to let Frank know." She grabbed Roxy's hand. "I can't let the law know where Frank is, or what name he's living under."

"If you tell me, I'll get in touch with him."

"Oh, would you? Thank you so much." Zee looked around. "I can't stay here, anymore."

"That's all right," Roxy said. "You'll come to my hotel with me."

"Oh God, Roxy," Zee said, "what would I do without you?"

"You won't have to find out, Zee," Roxy assured, and gave the woman a big hug.

Chapter Thirty

When Kelly came back in, he sat across from Zee and spoke in a low, well-modulated tone. Both Zee and Roxy could hear the people out front, shouting questions and accusations.

"Mrs. James," Kelly said, "who shot your husband?"

"His name is Bob Ford."

"Did you see him shoot him?"

"No," she said, "I was in the kitchen. But I ran in when I heard the shot, and Bob was standing there with a gun. When he saw me, he and his brother, Charley, ran out of the house."

Kelly looked at Roxy.

"What is it?" Roxy asked.

"She didn't see him pull the trigger."

"Is that going to be a problem?" Roxy asked.

"It might, if we take this to court."

"It won't be a problem," Zee said.

"Why not?" Kelly asked.

"I don't think Bob is going to deny it," she said. "I think he's going to brag about it."

"Well," Kelly said, "if he does that, we'll have him. Do you know where he is right now?"

"I'd guess he's in a saloon, bragging," Zee said.

"I'll have my men check," Kelly said. "Is he local?"

"No," she said, "he's like me and Jesse. He moved here a while ago."

"Staying in a hotel?"

"Yes."

"Do you know which one?"

"I believe it's the President Hotel."

"Not one of our best," Kelly said, "but not the worst, either."

"Captain?" Doc Willoughby said.

"Yes, Doctor?"

"Can I move the body?"

"Not yet," Kelly said. "I need my detective here, and I'm going to need more men." He stood up. "Mrs. James, do you have someplace you can stay? Perhaps some family member?"

"She can stay with me," Roxy said. "I'm just down the street at the Hanover."

"All right," Kelly said, "why don't you take her there. I'll come and let you know when your husband has been moved, when you can come back—"

"I don't want to come back here, Captain," Zee said. "Ever!"

"Well, that'll be up to you, Ma'am." Kelly said. He looked at Roxy. "If you take her out the back, I'll send Officer Bowen with you to keep people away from her.

But I have to warn you, once this gets out, the newspapers are going to be trying to interview you."

"Interview me?"

"They'll want to know everything about Jesse James," Kelly said.

"And what about you?" Roxy asked. "Aren't you going to want to know some things?"

"Yes," Kelly said, "I'm sorry, but yes, I will be asking more questions later."

"I'll be ready," Zee promised.

"I'm so sorry this happened to you, Mrs. James," Kelly said. "But you and your husband must have known his life might end this way."

"By violence, yes," Zee said.

"But not shot in the back," Roxy added.

"By a friend," Zee added. "A weasel, but a friend."

"The Fords were his friends?" Kelly asked, surprised.

"Charley rode with the James gang," Zee said.

"Not Bob?"

"No," she said, "but he said he wanted to. Then he does this. I can't believe it." Zee buried her face in her hands.

"Miss Doyle," Kelly said, "take her to your hotel and I'll see you both in the morning."

"Thank you, Captain."

Kelly stood up and yelled, "Bowen!"

"Yes, sir," the young officer said, coming out of the kitchen.

"Take these ladies out the back and escort them to the Hanover Hotel."

"Yes, sir."

Roxy helped Zee to her feet and they followed Bowen out the back door.

Kelly turned and looked at Doc Willoughby.

"My God," he said, "we've got Jesse James!"

Chapter Thirty-One

Roxy and Bowen got Zee to the hotel without encountering any newspaper people. Roxy got her a room and sat with her until she cried herself to sleep. Then Roxy went to her own room and sat there, stunned.

With Bob Ford shooting Jesse in the back of the head, did that mean he had shot her in the back, as well? She was going to have to find out.

Roxy wished she had a bottle of whiskey in the room with her. Bowen had wanted to come in, but she told him he probably should get back to the Thomas Howard house.

"Your boss is going to be looking for you," she said.

"You're probably right," he said. "I'll see you tomorrow, then."

After he left, she removed her boots, hung her gun on the bedpost, jammed the chair under the doorknob, and slept fitfully until morning.

***

In the morning she left her room to go to Zee's, and caught several men in the hallway, seemingly sneaking around.

"What the hell are you doing here?"

"Are you Lady Gunsmith?" one man asked.

"Was Jesse James really shot and killed yesterday?" another asked.

And the third said, "Can you tell us where Mrs. James is?"

"I'm not telling you a damn thing. Now get out of here before I put a bullet in your asses!"

They stared at her, but she actually had to draw her gun to get them to move. They turned, ran down the hall and down the stairs to the lobby. Roxy was sure there were going to be more of them milling around.

She went to Zee's door and knocked. The distraught woman opened the door and Roxy could see the fresh tracks of tears on her face.

"Are they gone?" Zee asked.

"I'm sure they're going to be in the lobby."

"Come in," Zee said.

Roxy entered and closed the door.

"Did you sleep at all?" Roxy asked.

"I slept all night," Zee said, "and when I woke up, I felt so guilty I cried."

"There's nothing to feel guilty about," Roxy told her.

"Look at me," Zee said. "I slept in my dress. I have nothing to wear."

"We can go to the house later and collect your things," Roxy said.

"I can't," Zee said. "I can't go back there."

"Then I'll go and pack a bag for you," Roxy said. "You can stay here. But maybe we better wait until Captain Kelly shows up."

"Oh God," she said, "he's going to have a lot of questions."

"Well," Roxy said, "he better have some answers, like where's Bob Ford? He better be behind bars."

"Ooh, I could kill him myself!" Zee said, closing both hands into fists.

"I don't blame you for that," Roxy said.

"Roxy . . . I don't know what to do."

"There's nothing to do but wait, Zee," Roxy said. "After Kelly asks his questions, we can go to the undertaker's."

"I—I'll have to buy a coffin."

"Yes."

"And Frank still has to be told."

"Just let me know where he is, and under what name," Roxy said. "I'll send a telegram. You said he's in Virginia?"

"That's right," Zee said. "A small town called Hurricane."

"Under the name B.J . . .?

"Woodson," Zee said.

"Right. I'll have to get to it later, after I pick up your clothes."

"And I guess I'll just . . . wait."

Roxy gave Zee another hug, and the woman held on tight until there was a knock at the door.

"Who is it?" Roxy called. If it was a newspaperman, she was going to shoot him—maybe just in the foot.

"Captain Kelly, and Detective Nelson," Kelly's voice called.

Roxy cracked the door, saw the two men, then opened it and let them in.

"Good morning, Mrs. James," Kelly said.

"Captain."

"This is Detective Nelson," Kelly said.

"Detective."

"We need to ask some questions."

"Of course."

"What about Bob Ford?" Roxy asked. "Do you have him?"

"We do," Nelson said. "He's in a cell."

"Good!" Zee said.

"But I don't know how long he'll be there," Kelly added.

"Why?" Zee asked.

"Well . . ." Kelly said.

"He claims he had a deal with Governor Crittenden to kill Jesse James," Nelson said.

"What?" Zee asked.

"You're kidding," Roxy said.

"We're not kidding," Kelly said.

"He's lying!" Zee said. "He must be."

"Have you checked with the Governor?" Roxy asked.

"We're doing that," Kelly said. "We sent a telegram to the Governor's mansion."

"We haven't gotten a reply yet," Nelson said.

"Look," Roxy said, "this can't matter, can it? I mean, even the Governor can't endorse a murder."

"Well," Nelson said, "we are talking about a wanted man."

"But a man," Roxy said. "And murder is murder. It's against the law."

"Did Jesse James know that?" Nelson asked.

"Jesse never murdered anybody," Zee said.

"Is that right?" Nelson asked.

"Look, Mrs. James," Kelly said, "we're not going to do anything until we hear from the Governor. And one way or another, this will all have to go before a judge."

"That's good," Roxy said.

"It might be," Nelson said.

"What do you mean?" Roxy asked.

"The Judge in this town," Kelly said, "is a Crittenden man."

Chapter Thirty-Two

Roxy got permission from Captain Kelly to go to the Howard house to collect Zee's things.

"I'll be back as soon as I can," she told Zee. "Just stay here, and don't open the door to anyone."

"Before you go," Kelly said, "we have some questions to ask Mrs. James. Would you stay while we do that?"

"Of course."

The questions had to do with when she and Jesse got there, where the name Thomas Howard came from, what they were planning to do in St. Joseph, what had they *been* doing during their time there.

Zee told them that she and Jesse intended to settle down. Jesse was putting his outlaw life behind him, and was going to start a new life as Thomas Howard. Roxy realized that some of what Zee was telling them were lies, and hoped it wouldn't come out in the end.

"I guess that's it for now," Kelly said. "We may be back with more later."

"I'll be here," Zee said.

Kelly turned to Roxy.

"We can walk you through the lobby. It's teaming with people."

"Thanks," Roxy said. "That might save me from shooting some of them."

"I hope so," Kelly said. He turned to Zee. "Mrs. James."

"Captain."

Nelson didn't speak to Zee as they left the room. Roxy wondered how much of the Captain's manners were real, and how much was put on. After all, as far as the law was concerned, they were dealing with the death of a wanted outlaw who was living in their town under an assumed name. They were being nice to Zee for a reason, which would soon become clear.

Captain Kelly and Detective Nelson walked Roxy through the crowded lobby, as newspaper men and women threw questions at her.

Outside the hotel there were more people, but as Roxy, Kelly and Nelson walked away from the hotel, the crowd thinned out.

"Miss Doyle," Nelson said, "I asked Bob Ford if he shot you, and he says he didn't."

"Do you believe him?"

"I do," Nelson said. "He also says Jesse was trying to put a new gang together, and that you were going to join him."

"That's not true," Roxy said. "I hadn't told Jesse yet, but I was going to turn him down."

"But were you friends with Jesse?"

"Not exactly," Roxy said. "I knew him, that's all."

"All right," Kelly said. "You might as well get Mrs. James some clothes. I have men stationed at the house, and they have orders to let you in."

"Thank you," Roxy said.

"We'll probably see you later," Captain Kelly said.

As he and Nelson began to walk away, Roxy asked, "Where's your Chief in all this?"

"He's been in Kansas City. We've notified him and he's on his way back."

"Is he going to be as nice about all this as you have?" she asked.

"That depends," Kelly said.

"On what?"

"On what the Governor has to say," Kelly replied. "You see, our Chief—"

"Is also a Crittenden man?"

"Definitely," Nelson said.

"I see. Thanks for telling me."

They turned and walked away, and she headed for the Howard house.

Chapter Thirty-Three

"Roxy!"

As she headed away from her hotel, she heard her name shouted across the street. When she turned she saw Bob Wolfe striding toward her.

"What the hell happened?" he asked. "I thought we were gonna meet up last night."

"Did you hear about Jesse?"

"Jesse James?" he said. "I thought that was a rumor."

"What about the crowd at my hotel?"

"I thought they were there looking for Lady Gunsmith," he said. "Jesse James was living in St. Joe under an assumed name? And now he's dead?"

"Yes."

"Jesus. Where are you goin' now?"

"Jesse's wife is in my hotel. I have to go to the house and get her some things."

"Well, you're gonna need your back watched more than ever now," he said.

"How do you figure?"

"This kind of thing can become an epidemic," Wolfe said. "Was he shot in the back?"

"Yes."

"And so were you. And it could happen again."

"You're probably right. Come on. I'll fill you in on the way."

***

By the time they got to the house, Wolfe knew the whole story about Jesse wanting to form a new gang, trying to recruit Roxy, and having the Ford brothers in place—only they killed him.

"What bastards," Wolfe said. "And cowards."

When they reached the house there was a small crowd still gathered outside, and two uniformed policemen on the porch. As Roxy approached, some newspapermen tried to block her path, but Wolfe shouldered them out of her way.

"Go on!" one of the policemen shouted at the crowd.

"Captain Kelly said I could go in and pack a bag for Mrs. James," Roxy told them.

"Mrs. James," the other, younger policeman said. "You mean that bastard Jesse James' woman?"

"His wife!" Roxy snapped.

"Shut up, Cates," the older man said. "Yeah, you can go in, but not him."

"I'll wait out here," Wolfe told her.

"I won't be long."

She went inside, but before going to Zee's bedroom she stopped in front of the picture frame Jesse had been fiddling with when he was shot. It was hanging crooked on the wall. She straightened it.

She went into Zee's bedroom, found an empty carpet-bag and proceeded to fill it with articles of clothing from her drawers and closet. Zee had a lot of dresses, simple frocks. Roxy hadn't worn one like them in years. There were also some trousers and shirts, and she packed them, as well.

When she came outside with the bag Wolfe was standing there, talking to the older policeman.

"Got everythin'?" he asked Roxy.

"I think so."

"Thanks," Wolfe said to the policeman, who waved.

"Do you know him?" she asked as they walked away.

"Turns out I do," Wolfe said. "seen him in the saloons a time or two."

"Did he have anything to say about Jesse? Or Bob Ford?" she asked.

"Only what you told me," Wolfe said. "I can't believe the Governor would condone murder—even the murder of a wanted outlaw."

"I can't, either."

As they walked back toward her hotel, Roxy said, "I have to make a stop."

"Where?"

"A telegraph office," she said. "Do you know of one that's not on a main street?"

"Don't want to be seen goin' in?" he asked.

"That's right."

"Yeah, I know one. Follow me."

He took her down a side street to a small, hole-in-the-wall office. And asked, "How's this?"

"Perfect." She held the carpet bag out. "Can you hold this and wait outside?"

"You don't want me to come in with you?"

"No," she said, "I'll be fine."

He said, "Okay, you're the boss," and took the bag from her.

She went inside and wrote a telegram to B.J. Woodson in Hurricane, Virginia, and had the key operator send it.

"If there's any kind of reply, can you bring it to the Hanover Hotel?"

"Yes, Ma'am."

She paid him, further depleting her paltry poke, and went back outside.

Chapter Thirty-Four

When they got to the hotel, there was a crowd outside, and in the lobby. Wolfe had to bull his way through, making a path for Roxy. The police had managed to keep people out of the hall, however.

She knocked on Zee's door. When the woman answered, she stared at Wolfe, curiously.

"This is Bob Wolfe," Roxy said. "He's supposed to make sure I don't get shot in the back again."

"That's good," she said, accepting the carpetbag from Wolfe. "Thank you."

"I'm so sorry this has happened to you, Ma'am," Wolfe said.

"Thank you," she said, again.

"We'll leave you alone so you can change," Roxy said, realizing that Zee's dress still had Jesse's blood on it. "Would you like a bath?"

"I would, but I can't go downstairs," she said. "Not with that crowd down there. I can see them out the window."

"Would you like me to bring a tub up here?" Wolfe asked.

"You could do that?" she asked. "I think I need to soak in order to get Jesse's blood off me."

"We'll make the arrangements," Roxy promised.

"I'll bring it up myself," Wolfe promised.

"Thank you both so much," Zee said.

Roxy and Wolfe left the room and went downstairs to get it done.

***

Wolfe carried a tub up, and then the hotel had employees carry up buckets of hot water. Roxy stood aside and watched as they filled the tub.

"Is that enough?" Wolfe asked her.

"That's fine," Zee said. "I can't believe it."

"Just soak, Zee," Roxy sad. "We'll be back later."

"Roxy," Zee said, as Roxy and Wolfe headed for the door, "did you send that telegram?"

"I did," Roxy said. "I'm waiting to get a reply."

"Thanks."

Roxy and Wolfe left the room and got out of the crowded hotel.

"Can't the police clear them away?" Roxy complained.

"It'll take some time," Wolfe said. "They're lookin' for somethin' to write. And I'll bet there are plenty of them comin' in from out of town."

"How about a beer?" Roxy asked.

“Sure.”

“I don’t have any money.”

“Oh, you want me to buy you a beer.”

“Yes.”

“Come on,” he said. “That means I pick the saloon.”

“As long as it’s not the Broken Branch.”

“Okay, but it’s not gonna be the Horseshoe, either. Whatever newspapermen are not in your hotel will be there.”

“I’m in your hands, then,” Roxy said. “Get me a beer.”

Wolfe took her hand in his and said, “This way.”

***

The saloon was called The Straw House Saloon, and it was on a quiet side street.

“They’ll never find you here,” he said, as they entered. “I come here a lot.”

“Wolfe!” the bartender yelled, as they entered.

The other patrons in the place turned and looked, and several of them exchanged a wave with Bob Wolfe. The interior was small and half full.

“Two beers, Henry,” Wolfe said.

“Comin’ up.”

Roxy and Wolfe stepped up to the bar and Henry set two beers in front of them.

"Who's your friend?" Henry asked. He was a large man with a big belly, and a smile to match.

"Roxy, say hello to Henry."

"Hello, Henry."

"Hello, Roxy."

Henry was going to say something else, but an expression on Wolfe's face convinced him to move down the bar and leave them alone.

"Nobody here is gonna bother you," Wolfe said.

"Good," Roxy said. "I need a few minutes."

"And if you want to get away from your hotel, my cabin in available."

She looked at him.

"I have other places I can stay."

"I appreciate the offer," Roxy said.

They drank down half their beers, and then stood there quietly for some time.

"You can ask," she said, then.

"Is it that obvious?"

"Since Zee asked me."

"So the telegram you sent was to Frank James?"

"Yes."

"Then he'll be comin' here."

“I don’t know,” she said. “I would think so, but I’m waiting to hear.”

“If he does come,” Wolfe said, “it’s gonna get very interestin’.”

“You’re right about that.”

Chapter Thirty-Five

Jesse James' death made Roxy certain of one thing. It hadn't been Jesse who shot her. There was no reason. And no matter how many times Bob Ford denied he'd done it, he was her best bet.

If she *knew* that Ford had done it, and that he would pay for shooting Jesse, she would have left town, satisfied. But if Governor Crittenden was going to somehow free Bob Ford, give him amnesty for the killing of Jesse James, there was no way she could live with that.

So she had to stay put until it all came out in the wash—and that meant possibly still being in St. Joe if and when Frank James showed up.

"What next?" Wolfe asked.

"I'd like to take you up on the use of your cabin," she said, "but I can't leave Zee alone. Not yet, anyway."

"You're bein' a good friend when she needs one," Wolfe pointed out. "But I better come with you, at least to get you to the second floor of the hotel."

"I appreciate that."

They finished their beers and walked back to the hotel. There was still plenty of activity out front, but it did look like the crowd had shrunk some.

"People might be gettin' tired," Wolfe said.

He still had to shoulder the way through the crowd in the lobby to get them to the stairs. When they got to the second floor, it was still empty.

Roxy knocked on Zee's door. When she answered, she was wearing a clean dress, her hair still wet from her bath. The tub of water, stagnant now, was still in one corner.

"Come in, both of you," she said.

"How are you feeling, Zee?" Roxy asked.

"Not better," she said, "but cleaner. Roxy, did you—"

"Hear back from . . . B.J.? No, not yet."

"We will. I know we will. He has to come."

"And do what, Zee?" Roxy asked. "Get himself arrested? What good will that do?"

"He's going to want to know who killed Jesse, and why. And then he'll want to do something about it."

"Well," Roxy said, "we'll see when we hear from him. Meanwhile, I don't want to leave you alone—"

"Oh no, I'm fine," she said. "You still have things to do."

"She has to find out who shot her," Wolfe said.

"Well, surely it was Bob Ford." She looked at Roxy. "You have to make sure he pays for that, and for killing Jesse."

"He will," Roxy said. "One way or another, he will."

"But if the Governor gets him out—" Wolfe said.

"He's not getting away with this," Roxy said. "No matter what the Governor says."

"That's right," Zee said, "but until . . . B.J. arrives or something else happens, you don't have to stay here with me every minute. I'll be fine. You go and do what you have to do."

"All right, then," Roxy said. "I told the telegraph operator to bring any reply back here. I'll tell the desk clerk to give it to you if I'm not around."

"Good. And you might tell him to have somebody come up here for this tub."

"I will," Roxy promised. "I'll be back here soon." Zee nodded, sat on the bed and folded her hands into her lap. Roxy wondered if she was going to stay that way the entire time.

She and Wolfe left the room.

"What now?"

"I want to leave the hotel, but I don't want anyone to know I left. Is there a back way out of here?"

"I'm sure there is," Wolfe said. "All hotels have back doors. It's just a matter of finding it."

"Then let's take care of that little matter," Roxy suggested.

***

They found the back door and left the hotel without anyone in the crowd being the wiser.

Roxy stopped abruptly and leaned against the wall of the building.

"What's wrong?" Wolfe asked.

"It's sort of hitting me now," she said. "I'm not sure what to do next."

"I am," he said. "Let's go to my cabin and you can get some rest."

"I should probably go over to the undertaker's office, make sure Jesse is . . . okay."

"He's fine," Wolfe said. "He's dead. Nothin' can hurt him now. Maybe tomorrow there'll be some word from Crittenden, or from Frank James. Then you'll have a clearer picture of what's goin' on."

"Maybe you're right," she said.

"Sure I am," he said, taking her left arm. "Come on. My place ain't much, but there's a bed and you can rest."

"Yes, all right," she said. "I did sleep fitfully last night, and a little rest sounds good."

Chapter Thirty-Six

When they got to his cabin, Roxy started to have a change of heart.

"There's still plenty of daylight left," she said.

"To do what?"

"I could go to the jail, talk to Bob Ford," she said. "Get him to admit he shot me."

"What would that accomplish?"

"Well, I wouldn't have to wonder, anymore," she said. "And once I'm sure Crittenden is not going to get Ford off, I could leave town."

"That can all still happen after you get some rest," Wolfe said. "It'll make your mind sharper."

"That's true."

"Come on," he said, tugging on her arm, "come inside."

They entered the cabin which, though small and crudely furnished, was clean.

"It's clean," she said.

"Noticing that for the first time, are ya?" he asked. "I don't like livin' in dirt, so I run a broom over the place a couple of times a week, and even dust."

"How unlike a man," she said. "Most men I've known don't see dust."

"Well, they've given you a bad opinion of us."

The bed was a surprise. It was a four poster.

"Where'd this come from?" she asked.

"St. Louis," he said. "It's the one thing I decided to spend money on when I moved in here. No matter what I do during the day, I want to have a good night's sleep."

She sat on the bed.

"Wow, this mattress feels good."

"Look," Wolfe said, "you can hang your gunbelt on the post, there. Easily within reach. Then kick off your boots and get some sleep."

"What will you do?"

"Sit in a chair on the porch," he said. "Keep an eye out for trouble. Make sure you're not disturbed."

"Why don't you lie down, too?" she asked.

"Roxy, when I offered, I didn't mean—"

"No, no," she said, "it makes sense. It's a big bed and you need rest, too."

"Rox—"

"I'm not going to lie down unless you do, too."

"Well," Wolfe said, "you drive a hard bargain. Let me go out and unsaddle the horses. They deserve some rest, as well."

She started to get up.

"I'll come with you and do mine—"

"Hey, hey, just relax," he insisted. "I can take care of both horses. Take off your gunbelt and boots and lie down. I'll be back in soon."

She started to reach down for her boots when he said, "I tell you what. Let me help you."

He came over, knelt down in front of her and first pulled off one boot, then the other, and her socks. When her feet were bare, he took her right one in his hand and began to rub it.

"Oooh, that feels good," she groaned.

"I know," he said. "I do it to my own every night. Here, give me the other one."

He lifted her left foot and began to rub it, bending the toes, flexing the ankle. At one point he slid his hand beneath her pant leg to rub her calf. She didn't complain. He did the same thing to the right.

"There," he said. He started to get up, but she reached out, grabbed a handful of his shirt and pulled him to her so she could kiss him.

"I told you," he said, "when I offered you my cabin, I had no ideas."

He stood up.

"I'll unsaddle the horses, rub them down, and then be back."

He went out the front door and she heard him walk the horses to the back, to the leanto. Abruptly, the picture of his bare butt came into her mind, and she knew what she needed even more than sleep.

***

When Wolfe came back into the cabin Roxy was lying on the bed, her gunbelt hanging from the bed post. He didn't want to wake her, so he moved quietly, did the same with his own gun, and boots, then got on the bed next to her. She was right. There was plenty of room for both of them.

Roxy heard every move he made, waited until he was lying on his back on the bed before moving. She rolled from her back to her right side, reached out to slide her hand up to his belly. Then down to his crotch. She found the bulge there and began to caress it.

"Roxy—"

"Shut up," she said. "You can't just rub a girl's feet and forget about it, can you?"

Chapter Thirty-Seven

She kept rubbing until he was good and hard before undoing his belt and buttons and sliding her hand in. His bare cock was hot as she stroked it.

And it was huge.

"My God," she said, "we have to get these pants off."

"I think so."

They worked together to get his trousers off, and then Roxy ran her hands over his muscular bare thighs. Then she slid his shirt up to expose his stomach, leaned over and peppered it with kisses. She winced at the pain in her injured shoulder, but didn't let that stop her. Instead of lifting the shirt higher, she unbuttoned it and peeled it off him. When he was completely naked, she slipped off the bed and began to undress.

"Do you want help?" he asked.

"Just stay where you are," she said. "I want to stare at you while I undress."

Actually, she was staring at his impressive cock as it stood straight up from his crotch. She couldn't get her clothes off fast enough, but was slowed down by her wounded shoulder.

He saw the bandage once she was naked, even though he found it hard to take his eyes off her large, heavy breasts.

"You have to be careful," he said. "You have stitches, right?"

"That's right," she said, "but if I lie on my belly, like this—" She settled down between his spread legs. "—I should be able to do this without tearing a stitch."

"I sure hope so."

"Well, let's see."

She began to stroke his cock with her right hand while kissing his testicles. With her left, she reached up and stroked his chest.

"Jesus," he gasped, as her fingertips touched the sensitive spot just beneath the head of his cock.

"Let me try this," she said.

She took her weight on her left hand, lifted herself just high enough to take his cock into her mouth. Lovingly, she began to suck, moving her head back and forth, allowing his penis to slide in and out.

She got to her knees, ignored what the move did to her wound, and wrapped her hand around the base of his cock while she continued to suck.

"Oh my God," he moaned.

Roxy groaned too as his cock grew even harder, and then she had to release it from her mouth so she could sit on it.

"Are you sure—" Wolfe started to ask.

"I'm fine," she said. "Better than if I was lying on my back. Now, just enjoy, because that's what I'm going to do."

She started riding him, coming down hard each time to drive the length of his cock into her. He began to move his hips in unison with hers, their flesh making slapping sounds as it came together. The air quickly filled with those sounds, as well as their grunts and groans, and the scent of their combined juices and perspiration.

She leaned over him so that he could mouth her nipples, which had become as hard as diamonds. When her orgasm rose up in her and overcame her, she thought she might have torn a stitch or two, but at that moment she didn't care.

Then he roared and exploded into her . . .

***

Later, she was lying on her right side while he was on his back, her left hand stroking his now semi-hard cock as it lounged lazily on his flat stomach.

"You keep that up, you're gonna start me up again," he said.

"I don't care," she said. "I've wanted to get you started ever since you showed me your bare butt that day."

"I wasn't sure you noticed."

"I noticed," she assured him. "Why do you think I had to step outside to keep from biting it."

"Ooh, can we do that, later?" he asked. "Bite each other's butts?"

"Definitely." Roxy was afraid she'd found a man, other than Clint Adams, who she wanted to have sex with, again. Usually, she fucked them and sent them on their merry way. That was so there was nothing keeping her from searching for her father—no other people in the picture.

"But I think we should do what we were planning to do before we got interrupted."

"What's that?" he asked.

"Sleep."

"And who interrupted us?"

"Yeah, yeah," she said, "I did. Never mind that, just let me get a couple of hours sleep before the butt biting starts."

"You got a deal," he said.

Chapter Thirty-Eight

Chief John Speelman looked at the men in his office—Captain Ted Kelly, and Detective Ed Nelson. He had just arrived from Kansas City, and his suitcase was behind his desk, still packed.

He was a large, barrel-chested man in his early sixties who had been lured from an Eastern post to head the new St. Joseph, Missouri police department.

"All right," Speelman said, "I want to know what the hell's been going on, and don't leave anything out."

He kept the two men standing while they filled him in on the Thomas Howard/Jesse James business, the fact that Lady Gunsmith was in town, and Bob Ford was in jail.

"And Ford said what?"

"That Governor Crittenden backed his plan to kill Jesse James," Kelly said.

"Then why is he in my jail?"

"Well . . . we haven't heard back from the Governor yet, to back his claim," Kelly said.

"But he shot a wanted killer," Speelman pointed out. "We should be pinning a medal on him."

"Uh, sir," Kelly said, "he shot him in the back."

"How else was he supposed to face a killer?" Speelman said. "And by the way, has Ford admitted to shooting him in the back?"

"He has," Nelson said.

"But with the Governor's support."

"Yes."

"Well, Crittenden usually knows what he's doing," the Chief said. "Now, what's this about Jesse James living in our town?"

"Yes, sir, as Thomas Howard," Kelly said. "In a house on Lafayette Street."

"That's ridiculous," the Chief said. "The man had a hell of a nerve, but I guess he learned the error of his ways, eh?"

"If you say so, sir," Kelly said.

"And what about Lady Gunsmith?" the Chief asked. "What the hell does she have to do with this?"

"Well," Kelly said, "She is apparently friends with Jesse James' wife, Zerelda."

"His wife."

"Yes."

"And where is she?"

"In a room at the Hanover Hotel," Kelly said.

"And why isn't she in a jail cell?"

"Uh, she's not wanted for anything, sir," Kelly said. "And she hasn't done anything here in St. Joe that we can arrest her for."

"She was living in our town with her bank robbing, train robbing, sonofabitch killer husband, Jesse James. What more does she have to do?"

"It wouldn't look very good for us to mistreat a new widow, sir," Kelly said, "no matter who her husband was."

"Huh," the Chief said, but didn't argue the point. "And where's Jesse James' body."

"It's with Simon Cruise, the undertaker," Kelly said.

"Have you talked to the Judge yet?"

"No, sir," Kelly said. "We've been waiting to hear from the Governor."

"And this shooting of Lady Gunsmith in the back," the Chief said. "Do we know who did it?"

"No, sir," Nelson said.

"What does Bob Ford say about it?"

"That he didn't do it," Kelly said.

"And do you believe him?"

"Well, since he admits to shooting Jesse James, why wouldn't he admit to shooting Roxy Doyle if he did it?" Kelly asked. "So yes, I believe him."

"And is she walking around?"

"Yes," Kelly said. "Doc Willoughby bandaged her up and she's okay."

"Then this is what I want," the Chief said. "I want her gone by tomorrow."

"Sir?" Kelly said.

"You heard me," Chief Speelman said. "Run her out of St. Joe, gentlemen."

"But—" Kelly said.

"No, buts," Speelman said. "I want her gone."

"The newspapers are going to want to know why, sir," Kelly said.

"How many reporters do we have in town since the James shooting?" Speelman asked.

"It's hard to count, sir," Kelly said. "There are crowds of them."

"If we run her out now," Nelson said, "they're liable to think it has something to do with the James shooting."

"I'm going to take what you say under consideration," the Chief said. "So for now, don't do anything."

"Yes, sir," Kelly said.

"All right," Speelman said, "I have some unpacking to do. I'll be at home. When we hear from the Governor, I want to know about it."

"Yes, sir," Kelly said.

Without further comment Speelman picked up his bag and left the office.

"Yeah, good job, men," Nelson said.

Kelly rolled his eyes.

Chapter Thirty-Nine

Roxy opened her eyes and immediately looked up at her gun hanging on the bedpost. Only after that did she look around the room, and then at the naked man lying next to her. She was also naked, a little cold at that moment. Slowly, she got to her feet and—careful of her stiff shoulder—got dressed, and then strapped on her gun.

She didn't know how long they had been in bed, but a look out the window told her it wasn't yet dark. Suddenly, she was very aware of the fact that she was starving.

"Sneakin' out?" Wolfe asked, from the bed.

"Not if I still want you to watch my back," she said. "You hungry?"

"Starved." He sat up, then swung his legs around and planted his feet on the floor. When he stood up, she looked at his naked butt, and this time didn't look away as he got dressed. When he turned and saw her watching him, he smiled. "Ready?"

"I'm ready," she said.

"How's your wound?"

"A little stiff, but if we tore any stitches, it wasn't too bad."

"I don't see any blood on your shirt."

"Good."

They left his cabin together, went to the leanto where he insisted on saddling both horses, and she let him. After that they mounted and rode back to town.

***

Arriving in town, they immediately saw the crowd of people in front of the Hanover, and knew there'd still be a crowd in front of the Thomas Howard house.

"Before we eat, I want to check in on Zee," Roxy said.

"You sure have taken her on as your responsibility," Wolfe commented.

"I like her," Roxy said, "and I feel sorry for her. She has no one here, no family, no friends."

"Until Frank James shows up," he pointed out.

"That's another thing I want to check on," she said, "whether or not there's been any word from, him."

They had to leave their horses off down the street, and then Wolfe had to use his bulk to forge a path through the crowd for her.

When they knocked on Zee's door, she answered it right away.

"He's coming!" she said, excitedly, grabbing Roxy's hands and pulling her into the room.

"Frank?" Roxy asked.

"Yes," Zee said, "he sent a telegram. Well, B.J. Woodson sent a telegram."

"What's it say?" Roxy asked.

"Three words," Zee answered. "On my way."

"What if somebody recognizes him?" Wolfe asked.

"Nobody recognized Jesse," Zee said, "I don't see why they should recognize Frank."

"Besides," Roxy said, "I don't think he's even wanted anywhere."

"Then why live in Virginia as B.J. Woodson?" Wolfe asked.

"He did that just so he could start over," Zee said. Then, bitterly, she added, "Which is what I thought Jesse and me were doing."

"I wonder when he'll be arriving?" Roxy said.

"That'll depend," Wolfe said, "on when he sent that telegram, and when he left Virginia."

There was a knock at the door, then, and Zee went to it.

"Who is it?"

"Officer Mike Bowen," a man's voice said. "I'm looking for Roxy Doyle."

Zee looked at Roxy, who nodded.

"I'm sorry to bother you Ma'am—" Bowen started as Zee opened the door.

"It's all right," Zee said. "Roxy's here. Come in."

Bowen entered and saw Roxy. He smiled, then saw Wolfe next to her and frowned.

"What's going on, Mike?" Roxy asked.

"Uh, the Chief is back, and I did some eavesdropping."

"What'd you find out?"

"Well," he said, "Chief Speelman is definitely a Crittenden man. He told Captain Kelly he wanted Mrs. James arrested, and you run out of town."

"What?" Zee asked. "Arrested for what?"

"What did the Captain say?" Roxy asked.

"He sort of talked the Chief out of it, at least for now," Bowen said. "He told him it wouldn't look good in the newspapers if they mistreated a widow—sorry, Ma'am."

Zee waved away either the comment or his apology, or both.

"And what about me?"

"Talked him out of that, too, for the time being," Bowen said. "They sort of agreed they got to settle this whole Jesse James thing first, before they figure out what to do with Lady Gunsmith."

Roxy looked at Zee and they were both thinking the same thing—Frank James.

"Okay, Mike, thanks for the information."

Bowen looked disappointed. Maybe he expected a bit more appreciation.

"Uh, sure," he said, "I got to go back to work."

Zee let him out, closed the door, and said to Roxy, "That young man's in love with you."

"Who isn't?" Wolfe asked.

Chapter Forty

Zee was hungry—which surprised her—but still didn't want to come out of her room.

"I don't want to have to fight my way through crowds," she said. "I couldn't take that."

"We'll bring you something," Roxy promised.

"Do you think they'll arrest me, eventually?" she asked.

"I guess that's going to depend on what the Governor has to say," Roxy said.

"I'm going to have to leave this room, eventually," she said, "even if it's just to go to the undertakers to arrange for Jesse's burial."

"I can do that for you, too, if you want," Roxy said, "or Frank may want to do it."

"If he rides into town as Frank James," Wolfe pointed out.

"I need Frank to be here," Zee said, "but I'm also afraid of what he'll do to Bob Ford if and when he sees him."

"Especially if they release him," Wolfe added.

"I still can't believe Ford made a deal with Crittenden to kill Jesse," Roxy said.

"Jesse was a thorn in the Governor's side for a long time," Zee pointed out.

"Yes, but if that gets out, wouldn't it be—what do they call it—political suicide?" Roxy asked.

"Or," Wolfe said, "it might get him into the White House."

"That's crazy," Roxy said. "Zee, we'll be back with some food for you."

"Thank you, both."

Roxy and Wolfe left the room, made their way through the crowded lobby and street outside, and away from the madhouse that was the Hanover Hotel.

"I thought they were thinning out last time, but now it looks like there's even more of them."

"This will be a big story for a while," Wolfe pointed out.

As they walked away from the hotel, Roxy said, "Do you know what I've been hearing?"

"What?"

"All about Bob Ford being in jail, and having a deal with the Governor."

"So?"

"So where's Charley in all this?" Roxy asked. "Zee said he was in the house with Bob and Jesse. Where is he now?"

"You're gonna tell me you have a guess, right?"

"That's right," she said. "I do. Come on."

***

Outside the Broken Branch Saloon, they stopped and peered over the batwing doors.

"There he is," Roxy said.

"Where?"

"The same table against the wall where I first met him and Bob," she said.

"So what do you wanna do?"

"Let's get a beer."

They entered the saloon and proceeded directly to the bar. The bartender who had called her "girlie" served them two beers without a comment. She noticed how warily the barkeep looked at Wolfe.

Roxy could see exactly when Charley Ford spotted her. He got quickly to his feet and headed for the doors, only she was there to intercept him.

"Hey, Charley," she said. "How you doing?"

"I'm fine," Charley said. "I gotta go."

"Where?" she asked. "To visit your brother in jail?"

"No, I—"

"Come on, have a beer with us."

"I really can't—"

"Wolfe!" she yelled.

Wolfe was by her side in a second.

"Convince Charley Ford, here, to have a beer with us at the bar, will you?"

Wolfe abruptly wrapped his arm around Charley's neck and said, "Come on, Charley. One drink."

"Um o-okay," Charley said, barely able to breathe. "One drink."

"See?" Roxy said to him. "It's not so hard to be nice, is it?"

"N-no, it isn't," Charley agreed.

Wolfe dragged him over to the bar, where they stood him right between them.

"Barkeep," Roxy shouted, "a beer for my friend."

The bartender brought it over, then hurried down the bar.

"Okay, Charley, pick it up," Roxy said, holding her own.

"Here's to Bob Ford," she said. "Big day for the Ford family, huh?"

"H-hey, look," he said, "I didn't have anythin' to do with that. It was all Bob."

"Bob, your younger brother?" Roxy asked. "He made a deal with Governor Crittenden to kill Jesse. You had nothing to do with it?"

"Exactly."

"Come on, Charley," Roxy said. "You were the only other one in the room when it happened. Describe it to us, in detail."

Chapter Forty-One

"I can't do that," Charley said.

"Why not?"

"Because Bob's my brother," he said. "I can't say anythin' that would hurt him."

"Hasn't he done something that's going to hurt you?" Roxy asked. "Did you want Jesse James dead?"

"No!" he said. "I rode with Jesse. And I would've ridden with him, again."

"So why would Bob do this?" Roxy asked.

"If he did this—"

"He's already told the police he did," Roxy said, cutting him off. "And he says he had the approval of Governor Crittenden. Do you know anything about that?"

"I don't," he said. "And if Bob admits to shootin' Jesse, that's up to him. But I can't tell you that he did. If you wanna kill me for that, Miss Doyle, go ahead. He's my brother."

"Jesse had a brother, too, Charley," Wolfe said. "What do you think Frank James is gonna do when he hears about this?"

"Oh Jesus, I don't know," Charley said. "Jesse was Frank's younger brother. I know how I'd feel if somebody killed Bob."

"So are you worried that Frank might show up here? And what he'll do if he does?" Roxy asked.

"Very worried."

"You know," Roxy said, "if Governor Crittenden does back Bob, he might be out on the street. Wouldn't he be safer in jail?"

"From Frank? Probably."

"So don't you want to do something to keep him inside?" Roxy asked.

"I wanna do whatever I can to help my brother," Charley said. "But don't ask me to give him up. If he gives himself up, that's a whole 'nother thing."

Roxy looked over at Wolfe, who simply shrugged.

"Okay, Charley," she said, "I'm not going to ask you to betray your brother."

"I can go?"

"Stay, go, do whatever you want," she said.

He started to push away from the bar, then stopped.

"Is Zee okay?" he asked.

"What do you think?" Roxy asked. "She's lost her husband."

"To a coward's bullet," Wolfe added, "because no matter how you look at it, shooting a man from behind is the act of a coward."

Charley just nodded, looked conflicted, but in the end, he turned and slunk out of the saloon.

"Betrayin' your brother, that's a tough ask," Wolfe said.

"I guess so," Roxy said, "but when Frank gets here, if he can't get to Bob, he might take it out on Charley."

"Well, like he said," Wolfe commented, "he rode with them. Maybe he and Frank are friends, and that'll be enough to save him."

"I don't think so," Roxy said. "Frank's brother is dead. I don't think he's going to care who used to be his friend."

"How well do you know Frank?" Wolfe asked.

"I met him a few years ago," she said, "but I haven't seen him since."

"So you don't know what kind of man he's become," Wolfe said, "at this point in his life."

"No, I don't."

"I think if I was Charley Ford," Wolfe said, "I'd get out of town."

"It'll probably be a couple of days before Frank can even get here," Roxy said. "Maybe both the Fords will be gone by then."

"If so," Wolfe asked, "would he hunt them down?"

"I think if the Governor arranges for Bob to go free," Roxy said, "Frank would probably hunt them forever."

"And would you help him?" Wolfe asked.

"I have my own hunt," she said.

"For your father?"

"Yes. And I'll have to get back to that, as soon as I discover for sure who shot me."

"You don't think it was Bob Ford?"

"I don't *know* that it was Bob Ford," she corrected him. "Until I do, I'm not leaving."

"Well," he said, "that suits me. I gotta say, watchin' your back so far hasn't been much of a chore."

"Not yet, anyway."

"I was talkin' about your bare butt—"

"I know what you were talking about," she said, lowering her voice, "but let's not talk about it here."

They looked around, saw that no one was watching them openly, but only stealing glances.

"Let's go," Roxy said, "before someone decides to show a backbone."

"Yeah, you're right."

They turned from the bar and walked to the batwing doors, Wolfe walking right behind Roxy. Anybody who wanted to shoot her in the back would have to fire the bullet through him, first.

Chapter Forty-Two

They went to the small café where Roxy had eaten with Zee, and then again with Wolfe. They ate, and then got some food to take with them for Zee. They made their way through the crowd again, but the group seemed to have gotten used to them and simply watched while some of them also ate food that had been brought in.

They went up to Zee's door and knocked.

"Thank God," she said, as she let them in. "I'm so hungry I was thinking about going out."

"That might not be a bad idea, Zee," Roxy said. "But we can put that off 'til tomorrow."

Roxy handed Zee the tray she was carrying, and Wolfe the bucket of beer. Zee took them to the bed. She sat, removed the covering napkin, then picked up a knife and fork and attacked the chicken and vegetables they had brought her.

"I know where this comes from," she said. "I can taste it."

"You're right," Roxy said. "Wolfe took me there, as well."

"Best food in town," Wolfe said.

"I agree," Zee said, suddenly looking sadder. "I never got to take Jesse there."

"Zee," Roxy said, "if you like, I'll go to the undertaker's with you tomorrow."

"I *would* like that, Roxy," she said. "I'd like to bury Jesse and then leave St. Joe before they decide to arrest me."

"Where would you go?"

"Back home to Little Dixie, in Clay County. At least the people there will be welcoming, and I can use my own name. They considered Jesse and Frank heroes."

"Will you wait for Frank before doing any of that?" Roxy asked.

"I'll try," Zee said. "I expect him in a day or two, so it should be possible." She bit into a biscuit and chewed voraciously. "I think I'm cried out, Roxy. Jesse would want me to get on with it, not sit around and cry over him."

"Maybe Frank will go back to Clay County with you," Roxy said. "He's not wanted anywhere since he's already served his time."

"That'll be up to him," she said. "I won't ask. He'd feel obligated if I did."

"Sounds like you've been thinking about this," Roxy said.

"What else is there for me to do up here?" Zee asked. "My other option is to leave here and take Jesse's body with me back to Clay County, and bury him there."

"That sounds good, too."

"But somebody might try to stop me," Zee said. "They'd take Jesse's body—"

"No, they won't," Roxy said. "If Frank doesn't go back with you, I will. I'll make sure you and the body get back to Clay County safely."

Zee stopped eating and looked at Roxy.

"You'd do that?"

"I would."

"But . . . what about your search for your father?"

"I can go back to that once we get Jesse buried and you settled," Roxy said. "You just have to decide which way you want to go."

"I will," she said, "once I've seen Jesse's body. That's when I'll know."

"Okay, then," Roxy said. "Why don't I come and get you early. We'll have breakfast, and then go to the undertaker's place."

"We can take you out the back way," Wolfe said.

"We?" Roxy said.

"Well, yeah," Wolfe said. "I'm still gonna be watchin' your back. We don't know if your shooter is still out there, or not."

"That settles it, then," Roxy said. "We'll both come and get you in the morning."

"That'd be great," Zee said. "Thank you both."

"When you've finished eating just put the tray aside," Roxy said. "I'll return the plate and silverware later tomorrow."

They left her to finish her meal.

***

In the hall Roxy said to Wolfe, "I think I'll stay in my hotel room tonight."

"Tired already?" he asked. "After the nap we had?"

"It was sort of a nap," she said, "and yes, I'm feeling tired from it. Aren't you?"

"Not exactly," he said, "although I have to admit, I could do with another nap just like that one."

"Well then," she said, "why don't you spend the night in my room, too, and we'll take several naps."

"Several?"

"Well," she said, "more than one, this time."

"And what about your stitches?" he asked. "We don't want to tear them."

Roxy smiled at him and said, "Stitches be damned."

Chapter Forty-Three

Roxy and Wolfe walked down the hall to Zee James' door, both of them on shaky legs. It had been a long time since Roxy had sex with a man a second time and, she had to admit, the decision was a good one. But in spite of the energetic sex they'd shared all night, they had managed to also get some much needed sleep.

Now they knocked on Zee's door, Roxy not looking forward to seeing Jesse James' body at the undertakers.

Zee opened the door, wearing a black dress that Roxy had packed for her.

"Are you ready for this?" Roxy asked.

"No," Zee said, "but let's go."

When they got to the lobby, the newspaper reporters who were lounging on sofa's, or against the wall, sprang into action and rushed at them with questions. As he had before for Roxy, Wolfe bulled his way through the crowd, sending some of them sprawling, getting Zee to the street.

Out there they were peppered with questions, but kept walking until the trail of reporters following them petered out.

"Once they figure out where we're goin', they'll be back," Wolfe said.

"Maybe we can get this done quickly," Roxy said.

Zee, walking between them, seemed to lose the strength in her legs several times as they got closer to the undertaker's, but they gave her their strength and kept her on her feet.

Upon a board nailed above the front door was crudely written: SIMON CRUISE, UNDERTAKER.

As they entered, a small, chubby man smiled at them and spread his hands.

"Ah, can I help you?" he asked.

"This is Mrs. Jesse James," Roxy said. "She'd like to see her husband."

"Ah, oh, very good," the man said. "I'm Simon Cruise, by the way, the Undertaker. Mr. James is back here."

Zee grabbed Roxy's hand and said, "Come with me?"

"Of course."

Wolfe remained where he was as the two women followed the undertaker into the back.

Jesse was laid out on a table, still wearing the same clothes he'd had on when he was shot. Roxy was grateful that the body wasn't naked.

"Ah, here he is," Cruise said. He seemed to preface every sentence he spoke with "ah." "Ah, I will leave you alone," Cruise said, and backed out of the room.

Zee moved up to the table and looked down at Jesse. She fixed his hair, then looked at Roxy.

"I'm going to take him home," she said, "bury him on his family farm."

"I'll go with you," Roxy promised.

"I appreciate that, Roxy," Zee said. "You're a good friend."

"I wish I could do more," Roxy said.

"You may not want to when I tell you something," Zee said.

"What's that?"

"Bob Ford didn't shoot you," Zee said.

"What? How do you know that?"

"Because I did."

Roxy hesitated a moment while that sank in.

"What?"

"Oh, don't worry," Zee said. "I'm a very good shot. I didn't want to kill you, I just wanted to keep you from joining Jesse's gang." She looked down at Jesse again. "Now none of it matters."

It mattered to Roxy. She had been wondering who shot her, and now that she knew, she couldn't decide what to do with the information.

Zee looked at her again and said, "I'm so sorry. I hope you can forgive me."

"Zee," Roxy said, "I have to think about this."

"I figured you would," Zee said.

"I'm going to leave you alone with Jesse for a few minutes," Roxy said.

She stepped outside, where Wolfe and Simon Cruise were standing, deep in conversation.

"What's going on?"

"You're not going to believe this," Wolfe said. "It all happened this morning."

"What's that?"

"Well, first Charley Ford was arrested," Wolfe said, "and then he and Bob were charged with first degree murder."

"That's great."

"Wait," Wolfe said. "They were brought into court first thing this morning, where they were officially charged—and then pardoned by order of the Governor."

"What?"

"It appears Bob Ford's deal with Governor Crittenden was to kill Jesse in return for a reward, and complete amnesty for both brothers."

"Oh, my God," Roxy said.

"Do you want to tell Zee, or should I?"

"I think you better."

Wolfe frowned.

"Is somethin' wrong?"

"Well, if you think what you just told me was a surprise, listen to this. Zee just told me that she's the one who shot me."

"What?"

"She was afraid I'd agree to ride with Jesse's new gang."

"So she tried to kill you?"

"No, she says she's a good shot, and did exactly what she wanted to do, just wound me. She figured that would keep me from joining Jesse."

"Well, good goddamn," he said. "What are you supposed to do with that?"

"She also said she wants to take Jesse's body home to bury, and I told her I'd go with her."

"After she told you she shot you?"

"No, before."

"And do you still intend to go?"

"To tell you the truth," she said, "I don't know."

Wolfe looked out the front door, where reporters were gathering, obviously to ask Zee what she thought of the Governor's pardon.

"I better tell her what's happened," Wolfe said, "so she's not surprised."

"Good," Roxy said. "You tell her, and when Frank gets here, I suppose I'd better tell him."

"What do you think he'll do?"

"What would you do if it was your brother?"

Chapter Forty-Four

When Zee heard the news, she wasn't surprised.

"Crittenden has always wanted Jesse and Frank real bad," she said, when she and Wolfe came out of the back room. "Why wouldn't he reward Bob Ford for killing Jesse?"

"But complete amnesty," Roxy said, "after the jobs Charley pulled with Jesse and Frank? Why not offer Jesse and Frank amnesty to begin with?"

"Oh, he hated them," Zee said. "He'd never do that."

"So what do you want to do?" Roxy asked. "Go out the back way?"

"No," Zee said, lifting her chin, "I'll go out there and tell those reporters exactly what I think."

"All right, then," Roxy said.

"Roxy," Zee said, "I don't expect you to go with me, not after I told you . . . what I did."

"Wolfe can walk with you," Roxy said. "I have some thinking to do."

"I expected you would," Zee said, and went to make the final arrangements with the undertaker.

"Is this what you want me to do?" Wolfe asked Roxy. "Stay with her?"

"You don't need to watch my back anymore," Roxy said, "now that I know it was Zee who shot me."

"I don't see how you could ever forgive her," Wolfe said.

"I may not," Roxy said, "but for now just stay with her until you get her back to her hotel room. Then it's up to you what you do."

"Okay, if that's what you want."

"It is."

Roxy waited while Wolfe walked outside with Zee, and she addressed the reporters to tell them what a travesty she thought this whole thing was. Then Zee lifted her chin again and walked through the throng of reporters with Wolfe at her side.

"Ah, Miss?"

She turned, saw Cruise looking at her.

"Yes?"

"Ah, are you the one they call Lady Gunsmith?"

"I am."

"Ah, well, I could give you a very good deal on a first-rate coffin—"

"And why would I want that?"

"Ah, well, with the kind of life you lead you might not have time to pick one out before you, uh—"

"I tell you what," she said.

"Yes?"

"Why don't you pick one out for me."

"Oh, I could do that," he said, "I surely can. Ah, how much would you like to spend?"

"Just put together your best and most expensive package," Roxy said, "and I'll be back for it."

"Ah, oh, that's wonderful!" he said, happily. "I'll take care of that right away."

When Roxy walked out the front door, there was only one or two reporters left.

"Look," one said, "that's her."

Two men fronted her with pads of paper in their hands.

"Miss Doyle, would you care to make a statement about what's happened today?"

Roxy still didn't know what she was going to do about Zee shooting her, so she wasn't sure she wanted to say anything supportive in print.

"I've got nothing to say," she commented.

She walked away from the undertaker's office, hoping that the man was inside putting together the most cxpensive burial package he had, because she never intended to go back there ever again.

Chapter Forty-Five

The Fords were on the street later that day. They spent time in saloons, being bought drinks.

Roxy didn't see Zee the rest of the day, but she went back to her hotel around dusk, totally disgusted with how St. Joe, Missouri was treating Charley and Robert Ford. It was as if they were conquering heroes.

Wolfe went back to his cabin, where he was possibly chopping some more firewood. He seemed to know that Roxy was not only done with Zee, but with him and the whole situation. Roxy, in point of fact, thought she was better off not spending any more time with him. She had to get back on the trail after her father. She just had to make up her mind about whether or not she would still ride with Zee to take Jesse's body home. Could she forget about what Zee had done?

When she entered the lobby of the hotel, she saw a man sitting off to one side, apparently waiting for someone. When he looked up at her, she saw that it was Frank James.

"Jesus, Frank—" she said as he approached her, then caught herself. "I mean, Mr. Woodson."

"It's Frank," he said. "I don't think anybody in this town is gonna recognize me. How've you been, Roxy?"

"I'm good," she said, "except for getting shot."

"Zee told me about that," he said. "I was just in her room."

"How'd you know she was here?"

"I saw her comin' back from the undertaker this mornin' with that feller, Wolfe. We been talkin' for most of the day. Then I thought I'd wait for you."

"Do you want to come back upstairs?" she asked.

"Why don't we find a saloon?"

"Well, the Horseshoe is the biggest one around," she said. "We could get lost in the crowd."

"That suits me," he said. "Lead the way."

***

When they got to the Horseshoe, it was jumping, but luckily the Fords weren't there drinking free beer. Maybe they had moved on to the Broken Branch.

Roxy and Frank got beers and found a table in a corner. Men watched her as she walked across the room and didn't give Frank a second glance.

Once they were seated, Roxy said, "Frank, I'm so sorry about Jesse."

"He knew the risks," Frank said. "We both knew we were likely to die at the wrong end of a gun."

"How've you been?" she asked.

"To tell the truth, not so good," he said. "I've been feelin' kind of lost, and I think this is gonna help me make some decisions."

"Like what?" Roxy asked. "About the Ford brothers?"

"Roxy, I told Zee and now I'm gonna tell you. I'm not lookin' for revenge."

"Then what are you looking for, Frank?"

"To tell you the truth? Amnesty."

"What?"

"That's right," he said. "I heard that Crittenden gave amnesty to Charley and his brother. Well, I did everything Charley did. Why not me?"

"So what are you saying?"

"I'm gonna surrender to Crittenden."

"Frank," she said, "they might send you to Northfield."

"I'm gonna make the deal with the agreement that I won't be extradited to Northfield, Minnesota."

Northfield was the last James/Younger bank job, that turned into a blood bath. If Frank was sent back there, they'd hang him for sure.

"You think Crittenden will agree to that?" Roxy asked.

"I hope so," Frank said. "I'm tired or runnin' and hidin', and I don't want what happened to Jesse to happen to me."

"When will you do this?" she asked.

"First, I'm goin' back home with Zee to bury Jesse," he said. "And to see my Ma. Then I'll start tryin' to contact the Governor. And if I have to go to Jeff City to see him, I will."

"I hate the idea of Bob Ford gettin' away with killin' Jesse," Roxy said.

"I hate it, too, but I've got to think about the rest of my life, now," Frank said. "If I kill Charley and Bob, then I'll be hounded forever."

"If you get the amnesty, where will you live?"

"I don't know," Frank said. "I'm just gonna take it one step at a time."

"Well," Roxy said, "I've got to say I'm surprised. But I wish you luck with the Governor. Do you really think he'll go for it? Zee says he hated you and Jesse."

"It was really Jesse he hated," Frank said, "not so much me. "What've I got to lose, anyway?"

Roxy lifted her glass and Frank clinked it with his.

Chapter Forty-Six

Roxy decided not to accompany Zee and Frank back to Clay County with Jesse's body.

She rose the next morning with the intention of leaving St. Joe. Doc Willoughby couldn't tell her what direction her father had gone when he left, but Roxy was going to guess west. That was likely the direction whoever had shot him took.

She decided to stop into the police station and see Captain Kelly one more time, just to settle things.

Mike Bowen was behind the desk, and quickly passed her through to Captain Kelly. He had apparently given up on any further interaction with her.

"Have a seat, Miss Doyle," Kelly invited.

She took the same one next to his desk that she'd sat in before.

"The Chief is in his office, but I'm going to save you the aggravation. He's a Crittenden man, and totally supports what happened in court yesterday."

"And you don't?"

"I do not," Kelly said. "Murder is murder, in my book. This is causing me to second guess my job, here."

"I don't think you should give up the law, Captain," Roxy said. "You're a good man. I was suspicious of how nice you were being to Zee James, but then I realized you're simply a good man."

"I thank you for that, but I'm not thinking about giving up the law," he said, "just being a lawman in Missouri. At least, while Crittenden is Governor."

"Oh, I understand."

"And you?" he asked. "Are you leaving Missouri?"

"Just as soon as I leave here."

"And did you discover who shot you?"

"I did."

He held up his hand.

"Don't tell me, I don't want to know. I just want this whole sordid business to end. If you're satisfied, that's all that matters."

"Thank you."

"And is Frank James in St. Joe?"

She remained silent.

"Quite right," he said. "Don't tell me, because I'd be duty bound to tell the Chief. I believe we're done here, Miss Doyle."

"Yes, we are."

She stood and they shook hands.

"I hope you find your father."

"Thank you."

She left his office and, with a wave of her hand to Mike Bowen, walked out of the police station.

***

After she collected her new horse from the livery stable, she headed out of town. As she rode by the undertaker's office, she saw a buckboard out front. Zee James was sitting on the seat, while Frank James and another man slid a coffin onto the back.

She rode over.

"Roxy," Frank said. "On your way out of town?"

"As fast as this new horse's legs will take me, Frank," she said. She looked at Zee. "I'm sorry, Zee, but I can't forget what you did and ride with you to Clay County."

"I didn't expect you to, Roxy," Zee said. "It was a terrible thing, and I'm ashamed. But I have Frank, and we'll get Jesse home."

Roxy looked at Frank again, noticing how much older he seemed than the last time she had seen him—and slept with him. Sometimes a hard life just took it right out of a person.

"Frank, I wish you luck."

"Thanks. Roxy," Frank said, "You, too, finding your father."

She nodded to them both, turned her horse, and left St. Joe.

***

Five months after the shooting death of Jesse James, Frank James got on a train to Jefferson City, Missouri to meet with Governor Crittenden.

Roxy read about it even later in a Denver newspaper. Frank James had been granted amnesty, but only after spending a year in prison, waiting for the decision. When he was released, he went to Oklahoma to live with and care for his mother.

Roxy Doyle continued her search for her father, and continues it, still.

Coming December 15, 2019

Lady Gunsmith

8

Roxy Doyle and the Silver Queen

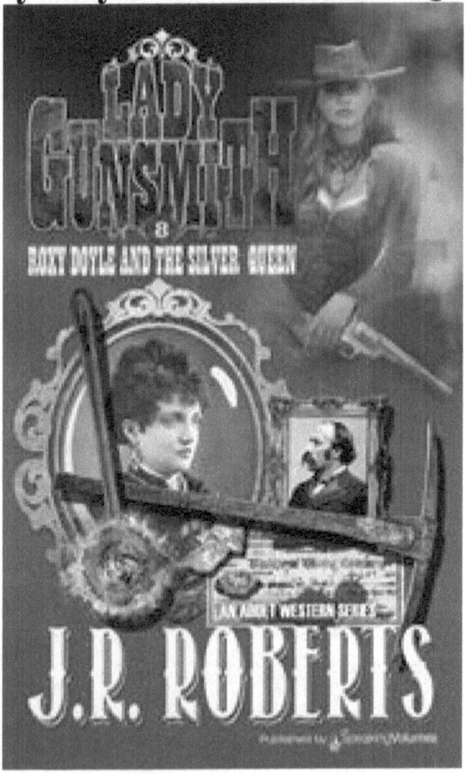

For more information

visit: www.SpeakingVolumes.us

Coming October 27, 2019

THE GUNSMITH
452
Portrait of a Gunsmith

For more information
visit: www.SpeakingVolumes.us

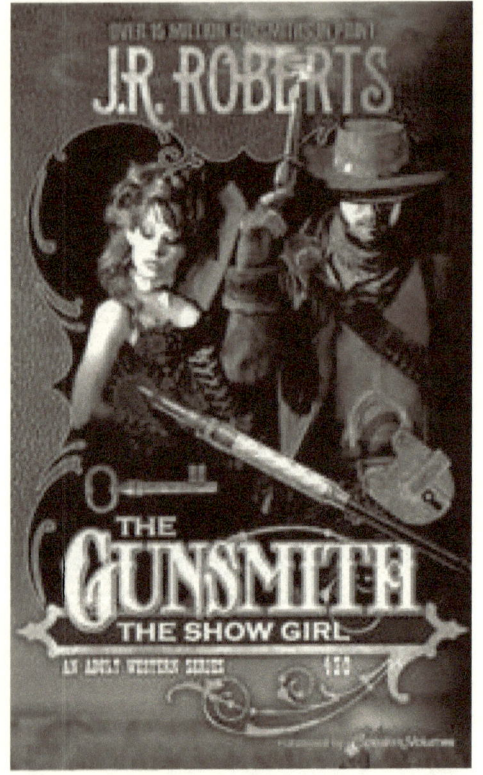

On Sale Now!

ANGEL EYES *series*
by Award-Winning Author
Robert J. Randisi (J.R. Roberts)

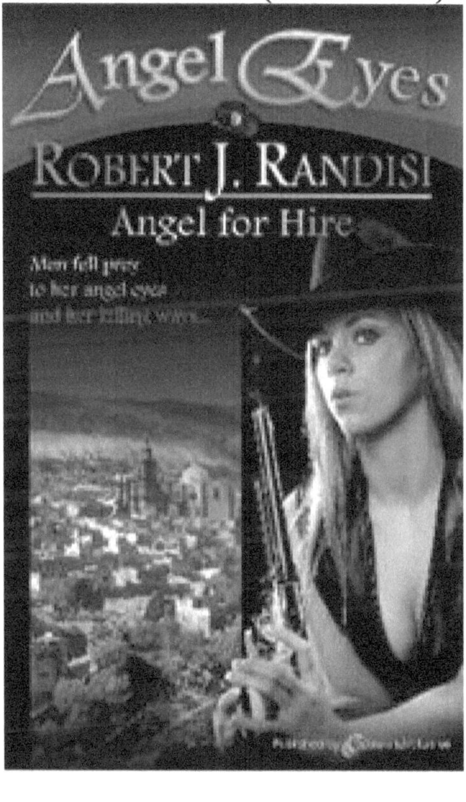

For more information
visit: www.SpeakingVolumes.us

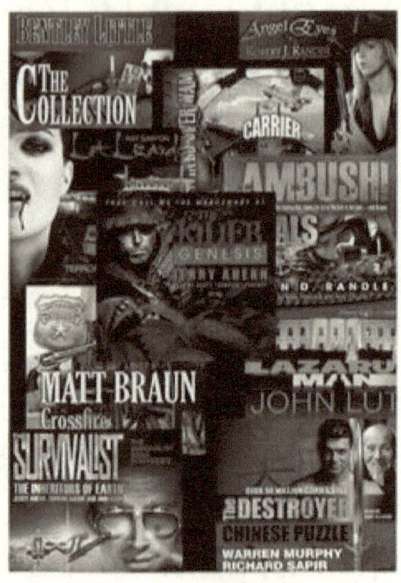

www.ingramcontent.com/pod-product-compliance
Lightning Source LLC
Chambersburg PA
CBHW030450250626
47154CB00003BA/1211
* 9 7 8 1 6 2 8 1 5 9 7 4 5 *